Cry of Hope

E. Chapman

Cry of Hope

Emily Chapman

WILLOW PLATE
PUBLISHING

Copyright © 2014 by Emily Chapman
Published by Willow Plate Publishing.
All rights reserved. No part of this book may be reproduced or transmitted in any form or by any means, including, without limitation, electronically or mechanically: photocopying, recording, taping, or storing in information storage and retrieval systems without written permission from the publisher.

Cover art: Ken Henley
Cover design: Ken Henley and Duffy Betterton
Interior formatting: Duffy Betterton / Web on Mission
www.webonmission.com

Scripture taken from 1599 Geneva Bible.

ISBN: 0615973124
ISBN-13: 978-0615973128

"O BEAUTIFUL FOR PILGRIM FEET,
WHOSE STERN, IMPASSIONED STRESS
A THOROUGHFARE FOR FREEDOM BEAT
ACROSS THE WILDERNESS!
AMERICA! AMERICA!
GOD MEND THINE EV'RY FLAW,
CONFIRM THY SOUL IN SELF-CONTROL,
THY LIBERTY IN LAW."

– Katharine Lee Bates

CHAPTER I

Discoveries

The road seemed endless. Hope glanced back at Mother and Father, who walked at such an unhurried pace it was infuriating. Did they not understand her impatience? She clenched her teeth.

Suddenly a thought struck her. Before it could slip away, she glanced back with a strange glint in her green eyes. Footsteps began pounding, *her* footsteps, and she silently refused to stop, though Mother called incessantly behind her. Capably taking in the narrow walkway, she took a deep breath of exhilarating air, trying to ignore the uncomfortable twinge of guilt far inside her chest.

Slowing only after Mother's calls faded, she then began to walk leisurely, swinging her arms in time with her cheerful gait. The Dutch homes lined one side of the walk, their brick fronts glistening in the sunshine; each were clean and neat according the scrupulous ways of the native Hollander housewives. The other side of the stone path dropped off to the canal of still waters that served so many purposes, not the least of which was delight for Hope's beauty-loving eyes.

Even now, as she spotted Constance's doorway standing just ahead, a sudden impulse overcame her eagerness to see her friend. She sat down with a thump on the sidewalk. Reaching a hand in, she trickled her fingers through the murky water. Her toes tingled. In a flash, her shoes were off; then came her stockings, and pulling up her petticoats, she dipped a toe in. She shivered at the cold rush that sent her blood flowing, and with a thrill of delight, she plunged both feet into the water.

She sat there in satisfaction for quite some time. The atmosphere was so peaceful she would have fallen asleep but for a cool breeze that rippled through, tickling her warm cheeks and loosening her knot of hair until it tumbled in dark waves down her back.

Suddenly her heart began to pound. A tapping could be heard, coming from around the corner. *Oh, dear!* She would be punished enough for running away, but to imagine what would happen to her if her mother saw her feet undressed! "Oh!" she gasped, as she fumbled trying to pull her long wool stockings on over her wet feet.

"Oh!" she whispered faintly again as a boot appeared. Suddenly, she found herself gazing up into the face of Joshua Mansforth, a close friend of her brother's. She sat back on her heels with an inward sigh of relief. However, though it was only a close family friend, Hope's face flushed with recognition of her unseemly appearance. Pulling on her shoes, she attempted to stand, but only managed to be in that awkward position between standing and sitting that is ever so precarious when one is a few short inches from a murky canal.

Joshua's face was grave, but his eyes twinkled despite his sober countenance, and he reached out a hand to help her. 'Twas a good thing he did, too, for had Hope not clutched it when she did, she would have fallen back with a splash and found herself in more trouble than ever. "Thank you." Hope dropped her eyes and bobbed a polite curtsy.

"Where might you be going?" Joshua asked. He bent down and whispered, "Running away again, Hope, eh?"

Hope's cheeks flushed. "Joshua! I'm coming to visit Constance." She gestured toward the doorway that stood just behind them.

"By chance, I appear to be going there myself. Father is here already." Joshua gave a cordial nod, which was so formal Hope giggled. "It seems there is a large meeting of which many are attending. Do you have any presumptions on what it is about?" He winked.

Hope sighed, "Mother tried to tell me, but I wasn't listening all too well. Has it anything to do with the New World?"

"Yes, it has everything to do with the New World," Joshua replied seriously. "I have reason to believe it may be one of the last ones concerning how we will get there. The preparations are many and our funds short, but we have found a solution through a man named Thomas Morton. If my predictions are correct, we may be leaving in fairly good timing."

Hope's mouth dropped. She had known, of course, that her elders had been planning a means of transferring to the New World and building a plantation. Yet it had seemed to take so dreadfully long, and she had only vaguely known exactly what was going on. It had simply seemed unreal.

With a start, she rushed past Joshua. Her heart was pounding as the blood rushed through at rapid pace. Her mind whirled, and she thought it odd she hadn't asked her friend the question that was throbbing in her mind. *Is Constance going? Is Constance going?* The words echoed in her ears while greeting Constance's aunt at the door, who, in turn, hustled her into the kitchen where her friend sat on a stool, surveying the meeting glimpsed through the other door.

"Constance!" Hope cried breathlessly.

"Hope!" she returned, her usual cheerful smile alighting her face. She ran to give Hope an embrace, but paused as she caught sight of Hope's flushed cheeks. "Why, what is it?" she asked, her bright countenance fading.

Hope gazed into her friend's dear face a moment. Her lips trembled. "The New World," was all that came out when she tried to speak.

She frowned. "Yes?"

"Constance!" Hope cried in a tone that could have been mistaken for a demand. "Are you going?"

Her friend's frown deepened. "Well, I have always assumed Uncle would go."

Hope sighed in relief. Suddenly she gave Constance a big embrace. "Good," she said with a smile. "Because I could not bear it without you."

Constance continued to look troubled, but Hope didn't notice, moving on to her sixteen-year-old brother. He sat on a stool in the parlor, leaning against the wall directly outside the door with arms crossed over his chest.

"Brother!" Hope exclaimed quietly, throwing her arms around his neck in mock exuberance.

John chuckled. "Hallo, Hope." However, he seemed distracted, and while giving his sister an embrace, his eyes were keenly focused on the meeting. Hope settled herself on the floor at his feet with full intentions to listen as well. However, as Constance settled herself down next to her, the two could not help but start up an amusing conversation. Soon, because conversations between two thirteen-year-old girls are seldom reserved, they were given a warning nudge by John. It became so lively, as a matter of fact, that they were escorted into the kitchen by Constance's aunt, Goodwife Robinson.

"Children, children," she clucked. "Why must you act so unseemly in the midst of perchance the most important meeting yet!"

"Most important?" Hope asked, sliding onto a stool. "Why is this one ever so much more important than others?"

"Did you not see the tall man in the middle?" Goodwife Robinson implored, waving her hand to the closed door. "'Twas Thomas Morton! He is a merchant with tremendous plans and has offered to sail us to the New World on account we set up a profit of fishing and share the proceeds."

"Did we accept?"

"Oh, dear me, child, we do not know yet! 'Twill take much prayer and petition to see if this is the good Lord's will. However, I have much presumption that our good men will be unable to pass it down. Our short funds exceed far below the tremendous amount the immense essentials would cost. Thomas Morton's offer seems fair, and though more work will perchance need to be done—well, we are not sailing to the New World to escape healthful work!"

Hope glanced anxiously at Constance. Her friend took the cue and asked her aunt, "Should we accept Master Morton's offer..." She hesitated, before blurting out, "I mean to say, you and dear Uncle and I would be sailing, no?"

Goodwife Robinson's face froze. Her brown eyes grew soft, and coming over to sit next to the two girls, she touched Constance's arm. "Dear child," she began, "you are now quite nearly fourteen years of age—practically a woman despite your childish deeds. I have kept you close by my side these many years, teaching you the notable tasks of housekeeping and all the other desired knowledge your mother wished you to have since you were but seven."

Hope touched Constance's other arm breathlessly, feeling oddly that Goodwife Robinson's speech was much longer than she had anticipated. Her stomach twisted.

"Your mother wished me to..." the lady's voice trailed off, but she composed herself quickly and said, "The fact is your mother entrusted me in your care after your father died until you were fourteen years of age. Then she wished me to return you to her."

Constance was silent for a moment, her blue eyes wide. "But, dear Aunt, what does this mean?"

"It means the New World is out of the question, dear."

Hope's fist clenched, and her clutch on her friend's arm grew fierce. "No!" she whispered. "No."

"Why did she not tell us beforehand?" Hope cried angrily, before choking on the tears that streamed down her face.

"What good would it have done?" Constance still

sat on the stool, as she had for an hour, moving only to brush away tears that threatened to spill in pools at her feet.

"So I could treasure my moments with you!" Hope paused her pacing and flung her arms in the air. "Or perchance we could have thought of something miraculous beforehand! But now... now, 'tis too late." Her shoulders slumped.

"I do not understand why she had not said my mother would wish to have me at age fourteen beforehand." Constance leaned her chin on her fist with a frown.

Hope paused as she saw the pain in her eyes, and she went to sit beside her friend. "Do you remember her?"

Constance's eyes were brimmed with tears. "Yes," she said, her voice strangely contorted. "It seemed she was always laughing. But then... then Father died. 'Tis strange, Hope. I do not remember her from then onward. 'Tis as if, with his death, my mother died as well. All memories of her from then on vanished. I cannot even tell when the memories stopped. It feels as if I have always lived with Aunt and Uncle. It feels as if she and he were mere dreams."

Hope stared at her. "Oh, Constance!" she breathed. She felt a pang in her stomach: a pang, not only from sympathy, but from something like empathy as well.

Constance propped her chin up on her fist. "I want to see her again, Hope, I truly do. What is she like now? Does she still laugh like she did then? Is her hair the same sunny shade of yellow? Does she... does she still love me like she did then? Sometimes, Hope, despite the lovely things of Holland, I wish she hadn't sent me here. Was she so very heartbroken when Father died... so very heartbroken enough to leave *me?*"

Hope was silent, unsure of what to say. Finally she

sighed, "Why *do* mothers send their girls away? It seems to me that learning how to sweep floors and bake bread is a terribly foolish reason."

Constance laughed, shaking off the despairing mood. "Hope, there is more to homemaking than baking bread. I should know as much." Her voice dropped. "I have been doing it for nearly seven years."

"Well, I am glad my mother has not mentioned a word of it as of late. My chores consist of washing the steps, serving the food, and folding fresh clothing."

"I am sure your mother will teach you." Constance smiled amidst the tears streaked across her cheeks. "Perchance she has a reason for waiting so long."

Hope shrugged. "She is simply busy," she replied ruthlessly. "'Tis this foolish New World deal, I suppose."

"Why then did she not send you to one of her dear friends to be taught domestic traits?"

Hope's green eyes grew cold as ice, and she said sharply, "She will not. I said as much. I cannot live without John, Constance, you know that as well as I."

"How obvious, Hope!" Constance gave a short laugh. "I shouldn't be surprised if everyone around knows how dearly you cling to him."

"Yes," was the short reply. "Because I love him."

A sudden silence fell over both, though their minds spilled over with thoughts. The conversation on love and parting had reminded them of the bond of friendship between them. However, both felt that, though they were still together, a gap had been set as their fate of separation had unfolded.

CHAPTER II
Lieve Vriends

"Hope, why must you have run off in such an unseemly fashion?"

It was Mother lecturing her daughter, who sat on a stool, her shoulders slumped as she felt a maddening sense of oppression towering over her. "I was desperate to see my *lieve vriend*," she replied with a hint of impertinence in her tone.

"I have doubts your desperation was as deeply great to see Constance as you say."

"'Twas pure disobedience!" Father cut in harshly, rising abruptly from his chair, his great frame towering over Hope.

She flinched.

Her punishment, though short as it was, was painful, for the rod never did come easily. However, she remained stony-faced through it all, though both her parents and John could not help but notice the fact that she kept a careful distance from any object meant to sit upon for several hours afterward.

Cry of Hope

As dusk settled down upon Leiden that evening, the hunched figure of Hope could be seen resting on the stoop of their home. The sun glistened between the tall neighboring chimneys across the canal, flashing every so often when Hope shifted. Father and Mother had decided her disobedience was enough to ban her from supper, so while she heard murmurs of talk and clanking spoons against iron, Hope sat rather disconsolately on the front step, trying to convince herself she did not mind but failing entirely. Her stomach began eating away at her ribs, and she was convinced she would not last the night without food.

"*Goedendag*, Hope Ellison!"

The cry caused Hope to look up with a start, and her face broke into a grin as she saw Jan, the bargeman, inching his way up the still canal on his flat barge, his crates now filled from his trip to the farmland.

"*Hoe ga je vergaat?*" Jan asked kindly, his pale blue eyes looking keenly into hers.

"I am faring well. Are you much better after your bout of fever?" Hope asked, though the words rolled off her tongue in fluent Dutch.

"*Ja, ja!*" Jan nodded his head vigorously, his eyes bright.

Hope smiled at his exuberance, feeling quite as relieved as he.

The barge came slowly inching past, rippling the calm water ever so slightly, causing it to twinkle as it soaked up the last few drops of daylight. Jan nodded to Hope as he passed, touching a hand to his blue cap and saying cheerfully, "*Goedendag!*"

"Fare thee well!" Hope cried back, waving her hand.

"Good day, Jan!" It was a strong voice from behind Hope.

Jan grinned and nodded as his barge disappeared behind a row of houses. His voice could be heard saying, "*Ja, ja*, John!"

"How might you be faring, Hope?" John asked, as he stretched out his long legs, sitting down on the step next to her.

Hope gave him a longing look, and John laughed, "No, no, little sister, I have helped you out of predicaments much too often. 'Tis quite time you take it on your own two legs."

Hope opened her mouth to beg and plead, but John reached out two fingers and closed it gently, saying, "Come now, Hope. Suppose I could not help you anymore? What would happen to you?"

"Nothing. Absolutely nothing."

"Oh?"

"Yes. You see, I would die. Then nothing would happen to me, absolutely nothing."

"Ah," John grinned. "Sounds fair enough. I shall stay close to you, and you will live for me. Correct?"

Hope laughed. "I suppose so." Reaching out, she dipped the toe of her shoe in the canal and flicked it up swiftly. Droplets of water flew into the air, sparkling crimson and gold against the sunset sky, before sprinkling down upon John's dark head. He gave a short little yelp in surprise, and Hope doubled over giggling at her comic.

However, John was not in any way slow, and the next instant her brown petticoat had dark splatters upon it. She shrieked and cupped her hands, splashing out a large dose of water onto John's boots. This time he gave another yelp, and the surprise that sprang up in his brown eyes caused Hope to

11

laugh so hard she fell gasping on the steps. "Oh, John!" she cried. "You should have seen yourself!" Crossing her eyes, she did a mock imitation of his yelp, drawing it out longer and sounding so utterly ridiculous she could have been mistaken for a hysterical hen.

John laughed and tweaked her ear, saying, "I have very high doubts I looked that way—or sounded that way for that matter."

"Oh, John, look at your poor boots!" Hope pointed to the wet leather that was stained dark.

"My poor boots?" John asked, with an indignant look on his face. "You say poor boots? Such a strange thing you should mention them sorrowfully now rather than before. It would have saved a dreadful lot of trouble, would it not?"

Hope grinned. "Yes," she said, "but it would not have been nearly as amusing."

"For you, perhaps, little sister," John said. "Now I must go in and place these by the hearth to dry." He frowned and stood up.

"Wait!" Hope cried, reaching out to tug on his coat.

"What is it?"

"I... I need to talk to you."

With a heroic sigh, John sat down again. "What deep subject must we speak on this time, little sister?" he asked, leaning his elbows back on the step behind him and assuming a most comfortable air.

Hope hesitated, and she bit her lip.

John reached over and tweaked her ear. "What is it?" he asked more gently this time.

Hope heaved a sigh. "The New World."

"Northern Virginia."

"What?"

"'Tis Northern Virginia. We are settling in Northern Virginia."

"Without Constance," Hope replied dully.

Understanding dawned in John's brown eyes, and he replied softly, "I had forgotten."

"I hadn't."

John was silent for a moment. "Hope," he said, "we are all going to feel our friends' absence dreadfully. 'Tis hard on Mother and Father as well."

Hope gave a soft snort.

"'Tis the truth," John said sharply. "Pastor Robinson is a dear friend to us all."

"Constance is my *lieve vriend*."

"I know," John replied, his voice growing soft. "She is more a sister to you than a friend."

Hope's eyes blurred, and she fiercely wiped the tears away. She commanded herself not to cry, but her stern wishes fell away as they began to run freely.

"Do you know Elder Brewster is leaving Jonathan and his sisters behind? Think how dreadful 'twould be if Father chose to leave me behind and take merely you and Mother. Or suppose he thought it unsafe to take you and Mother and went alone, leaving you both in my care?"

John's speech did little to comfort Hope, and the tears fell fast before her. Her grief, rather than lessening, deepened by the minute, and all of John's comforting did more harm than good. Her thoughts clung to an image of Constance, who seemed to shrink further and further away by the minute. Longing suddenly scalded her heart, as she thought again of her familiar homeland. She'd never be able to say "good day" to Jan again; she'd never be able to sit on the steps in the evening, watching the sun lower behind the chimneys and glisten on the canal. She'd never be able to see her dearest friend again. Her stomach began to churn at the last thought, and her mind whirled as she shook her head violently, as if it would ward off the fate of leaving.

Suddenly she heard John whispering in her ear, "'Twill be alright, little sister." His hand went up, roughly stroking her dark hair. "'Twill be alright."

"How many mufflers do we need?" Hope whispered to Constance a few days later. She and her mother were attending a little knitting bee, organized by all the women from the church to knit items needed for the small congregation sailing to Northern Virginia.

Constance giggled. "Have you not noticed they have given you and I the task of knitting mufflers simply to keep out of the way?"

"Are we such a nuisance as that?" Hope frowned.

Constance shrugged. "They choose to give us easy work while taking the difficult tasks upon their shoulders. 'Tis not such a terrible idea in my opinion." She winked.

Hope laughed, "Ah, you are such a cunning child! Much to my great fortune, I know not how to knit those difficult pieces they seem to enjoy."

Constance glanced at her. "Perchance I could teach you. Would it not be great fun to knit a complicated piece to surprise them?"

Hope sighed, "'Twould be, but I shan't know where to

start. Besides, 'twould probably turn into a bundle of trouble, for I am a dreadfully hopeless homemaker."

Constance's face contorted, and Hope said airily, "Oh, you may smile if you wish. I do not care all too much. In fact, I would rather not be a wife and mother at all. Let us both purchase a barge-house and live on the canal rather than home keep."

Constance shrugged. "I would prefer to stay home. I love to cook, and darling babies bring me such great joy, I would not mind a bit if they were the means of keeping me here."

Hope squirmed. "Babies *are* darling," she admitted, "but since I do not know a thing about homemaking, 'twould be a much easier ambition."

Constance looked at her, and a smile played around her lips. "Hope, do you know anything about handling a barge?"

Hope's cheeks turned crimson. "I suppose not," she said sheepishly.

Constance suddenly laughed warmly. "Oh, Hope Ellison, you have such a flighty spirit! You amuse me so!"

Hope knitted her eyebrows together. "Am I to take that as a compliment or insult?"

"Neither," Constance replied simply. "Merely take it as an arsy varsy way of saying 'I love you'."

Hope grinned, but her face fell a moment later as she remembered the reason for the knitting in the first place. Constance seemed to be thinking the same thing for her usually cheerful countenance was dismal. The sunshine pouring through the window behind them alighting their work seemed to cut through Hope's heart, and she wondered why it must to be so cheerful at such a time.

"Huzzah, there's John!" Hope cried, for during the last hour of the knitting bee she had been keeping her eyes peeled for her brother to escort her and Mother home. The knitting was wearying, and though she longed to be near her dear friend as much as her last precious few months in Holland would permit, her stomach disagreed to staying without refreshments.

Her knitting needles dropped to the floor in a clatter, as she practically flew to the door to let him in. "Dearest brother!" said she, as she flung the door wide and leapt to throw her arms around his neck.

John threw back his head and laughed, grabbing her around the waist and tossing her as high as the low ceiling would allow without mishap. "Little sister!" he grinned, as Hope shrieked in horror and delight at his actions. Her feet landed on the floor with a thud, causing every woman in the parlor to start and turn a disapproving stare upon Hope and her brother.

"What sort of rambunctious lot are the two of you?"

Hope turned to see Constance leaning against the doorway with crossed arms, grinning over the whole scene with an amused expression.

Mother must have felt it her duty to lead her two turbulent youth out of the bee, for she bid farewell swiftly and hustled them out.

"Will I see you tomorrow, Constance?" Hope asked anxiously, as her mother gave her a push out the door.

"I will try as I might!" Constance called after her as the door closed with a thud.

Down the familiar walk went the three: two merry and one sober. John and Hope laughed and jested as they went along, but very quickly the light topics folded into a serious one, as Mother and John began conversing about the voyage.

Hope, knowing little to nothing or perhaps a bit of both concerning the topic, was quiet as she walked slowly along beside her brother. "Did you know Goodman Danford has finally come to a positive decision regarding sailing to Northern Virginia?" Mother asked her son. Allowing no answer, she flew to saying, "Goodwife Danford announced today that he, after much prayer, made the verdict to come, bringing along her and their only daughter, Patience."

The last name brought upon a rather strange reaction by Hope, for when John glanced down at her, her face had distorted appalling. In fact, her tongue stuck out with such an unappealing appearance that it would have resulted in rather dire events had someone rounded the curve just then. John, used to his sister's radical oddities, grinned and whispered in her ear, "The dreadfulness of this voyage is deepening."

Hope crossed her eyes at him, but he simply chuckled, bringing upon a disapproving look from his mother, who had been entirely oblivious to the whole scene, being on the opposite side of tall John than Hope.

Dreadfulness indeed! Hope thought indignantly, *'Tis worse than dreadful. 'Tis hideous!*

CHAPTER III
Time is Scarce

The months seemed to have sprouted wings and taken flight when Hope learned she would soon be on a ship bound for Northern Virginia. Day by day, week by week, the time seemed to have no steady landing, constantly slipping by her with sly intentions, tripping her up every now and then with a nasty sneer, smacking her headlong with shock at how quickly it could fly past her. Though most of the preparations were taken up by her elders, Hope felt she had plenty of wearying time from the mere weight of the voyage that settled like a cloud over her shoulders.

It was dreadful being left at home with chores or lessons. Her last bit of time in Holland was drying up before her very eyes, and Hope felt she should be allowed more time than usual with Constance. However, her worried Mother could hold up a strict fortress, and her fussing and flighty ways could bear a wall firmer than might be expected. Hope tried all her ways to slip by that steady ground, but it never broke, and she found herself piled with more chores and more lessons than ever before. So she pressed her lips together in angry defeat and scrubbed away at the front steps so fiercely the brick glistened or scribbled away with a quill pen the lessons Mother set to her until the paper smoked and the pen smoldered and her work just barely slipped past Mother's sharp eyes with the less-than-perfect handwriting.

After her chores were complete, she slipped out the front door and raced down to Constance's house before Mother could think of any other task to assign of her. Oftentimes she would meet her halfway, occasionally nearly bumping noses with her as they simultaneously rounded a corner. They would then giggle merrily and link arms, chattering cheerfully or jesting with one another like two gleeful little fools. Several times they would walk toward the dikes and gaze out over the ocean, for both enjoyed the awesome sight and the salty breeze that blew their hair and settled on their lips. Other times they would hike a few miles until they came to their favorite garden, nestled between two darling cottages, complete with a windmill and stone bridge and beds and beds and beds of tulips.

That was the average day for Hope, and she, though being not overjoyed, soon came to realize the comfortable luxury she lived… much sooner than she wished.

Hope gazed in despair around the bare room. The small kitchen was dismally empty, the hearth cold, and the cozy little nook where her feather bed still nested seemed foreboding as it whispered in the stillness, "Here you no longer belong. Your fate lies in the New World. Your fate lies in the New

Cry of Hope

World. Your fate lies in—" Hope covered her ears and turned, running from her home. Tears began to stream down her face. Her home was no longer welcoming. It was no longer *home*. It was a dark, foreboding symbol stating she was an outsider, and her heart beat rapidly, longing to rebel against it but knowing she could not. She had no power over this fact, and she shivered knowing her helplessness.

She collapsed on the step outside, and sat there, allowing her trembling body to slow its trembling and wiping her tears away with clammy fingers. The July sun warmed her body, and she began to feel calmer.

"How are you faring, little sister?" John asked, sitting on the step next to her. The few belongings they were taking to the New World were nestled near the edge of the canal, waiting to be picked up by Jan and his barge. He was to take the entire congregation to Delfthaven where the *Speedwell*, the ship to take them to the New World, awaited.

"How do you suppose I am faring?" Hope asked, rather sharply, and rubbed her wet eyes miserably.

"I rather think you are faring poorly," John said with a smidgen of sarcasm rubbed in, "but I suppose that is not uncommon."

Hope glared at him, but her eyes caught sight of Jan rounding the bend, his barge carrying Goodman Danford, his small family, and their bit of supplies. Hope's keen eyes quickly singled out Patience, a girl near her age, who sat with her mother on their trunk and whose red curly hair blew in the breeze. *As unruly as Patience herself*, Hope thought with a sniff. The dislike was mutual, for Patience didn't exert herself in attempt to speak to Hope, and both kept a severe distance from one another.

"The Robinsons are around the bend a short way," John said to cheer his sister up once Jan started off.

For a moment, her heart leapt; then she remembered she would have but little time left with her friend, and her high spirits crushed dismally again. Several tears would have dropped on her lap had she not noticed Patience's steady stare, as if expecting her to begin sobbing. Hope, feeling rebellious at the moment, decided to disappoint her and swallowed down every choking tear that arose in her throat.

The Robinsons' doorway stood just ahead. Her spirits threatened to rise again, for Constance was coming with them to see them off at Delfthaven; yet suddenly they took a nosedive when she realized with a start Constance wasn't standing outside the door. Only her uncle, Pastor Robinson, was seen, and Hope's temples began to throb in true fear. Where was her friend?

The barge slowed to a halt, and Pastor Robinson stepped aboard, his ever-faithful companion, the leather Bible, in hand. Murmurs of greetings rose from all sides of Hope, but she leapt to her feet. "Where is Constance?" she demanded, causing Mother's hand to fly to her throat and Father to give a muffled growl in reproof.

Pastor Robinson's eyebrows flew up in surprise at her outburst, but he said gently, "The dear girl has developed a sore throat, and her aunt did not wish for her to sleep out in the damp air by the harbor tonight lest it become worse."

Hope waited not to hear more, but pushed past the sober man and burst into the house. "Constance!" she cried out in a strangled sob. "Oh, Constance, where are you?" And her breath began to come in gasps, her chest heaving.

"I am here, Hope," a soft voice came from the parlor,

and Hope turned. Constance sat by the hearth, a woolen blanket draped around her shoulders. Hope never forgot the image of her dear friend sitting there, illuminated by the golden firelight, her soft brown hair draped in folds around her shoulders. Her blue eyes glistened with tears, and they rolled slowly down her pink cheeks.

"Oh, Constance!" Hope whispered and fell on her knees beside her friend.

The two embraced one another for a long while. The tears glistening in Hope's eyes began to drop violently on Constance's soft hair, streaking it with bittersweet droplets that glowed in the firelight. Neither wished to be the first to let go, so they clung to one another desperately, as if physical clutch would remove the fate set for them and twist things back to the sweet original order. Their hearts squeezed when they realized that the other would soon become a memory, and that fact caused the bitter tears to fall thicker and faster.

"I shall miss you, Hope Ellison," Constance whispered faintly at last.

"Oh, Constance, I love you so!"

"Ah, Hope, but not so much as I love you!"

And their embrace became so strong that neither would have been able to let go had John not come in and gently but firmly removed Hope's clutch. "John, no!" she gasped, grabbing Constance's hands as he tried to pull her away.

"Come now, Hope," he said softly, tearing her hands from Constance's.

"Constance!" she cried, wildly trying to rush back to her friend, but John had picked her up and began carrying her out of the room.

"Oh, Constance, I love you!" she whispered faintly,

and she wrenched her head around, her vision locking with Constance, whose eyes were so full of love and longing that the image burned fiercely in Hope's mind with a permanent sear.

CHAPTER IV
Bitter Tears

Hope opened her eyes. Her vision exploded in oranges and yellows and faint tinges of pink, framed by the rooftops lining the canal. She blinked, wondering how the sun could give up to the night so soon, before reigning in its plethora of colours for a significant while. Yet, somehow, it never seemed to surrender entirely. The stars peeked through the night's thick shadows, as if light possessed a determination that refused to back down no matter how dark the world became. She rubbed her swollen eyes in wonder.

"What is it you find so fascinating to contemplate for *three whole minutes* after you've awakened?" a voice above her asked with amusement penetrating the mock seriousness of the tone.

Hope's eyes darted up, and she saw John grinning at her, his soft brown eyes alert. "Has she by any chance been wondering how a girl such as herself, with bountiful youth and zest, happened to fall asleep? 'Tis unlike her, unlike her fully," John said, smiling, but Hope caught the excited tremor in his voice.

"You are eager for the New World, are you not?" she said, as the fact suddenly seeped consciously into her brain.

John grinned. "And why should I not, may I ask? 'Tis a life of adventure, a life of new beginnings!" His voice began to swell in clear, eager tones. "Why, we will have the chance to start a new country! Our own haven of *freedom!*" He threw a fist into the air in his enthusiasm, venting out a bit of the excitement he had managed to keep contained for many months. Now the actuality of it all seemed to affect him in the extreme as well, only in an entirely different way than Hope. She knitted her eyebrows together. How frustrating.

She opened her mouth to speak, but suddenly the barge emerged in the bustling harbor, causing her to sit up abruptly, pushing stray hairs out of her eyes. A swarm of childhood memories threatened to choke her for a moment, but John placed a reassuring hand on her shoulder. She took a deep breath.

Struggling to stand, she held tightly to John's shoulder as she caught a glimpse of the familiar ocean. Grey, choppy waters, mixed with the sunset's enchanting rays sent clashing images to her eyes, adding to the dizzying affects of the harbor. She barely noticed the barge had bumped against the edge of the canal until Mother gave her a slight push.

The next thing she knew she was standing on the busy wharf. John rested his elbow on her shoulder, and they both gazed at the horizon for a brief moment. Hope felt sick.

Suddenly she glanced back, sensing Father behind them. His gray eyes stared at the same horizon for an instant, and she turned away, biting her lip. After a brief moment of tense silence, John was gruffly bid to help unload the trunks.

Cry of *Hope*

She then rested against a pile of crates, tilting her chin back as she stared at the darkening sky.

Before long, the barge was empty of belongings, and Jan was preparing to leave. He shook hands violently with the congregation, wishing them all good fortune on their "quest for ultimate freedom," in his Dutch way. However, his keen sight caught Hope in the shadows, and he approached her, his pale blue eyes glistening in the harbor torchlight. "Ah, Hope Ellison." He knelt down, tapping her chin.

She looked up, revealing her tear-streaked face.

"*Ik zal je missen,*" he said, pinching her chin in friendliness.

She swallowed. "I shall miss you as well."

He gazed at her for a moment before tousling her hair and saying, "*Nu, nu, op te vrolijken, zon!*"

She took a deep breath and managed a short smile. Wiping her nose, she stepped out and slipped her hand into John's, as Jan boarded his barge and slowly inched away.

"Farewell, Jan!" she cried out suddenly, just as he rounded the corner. And as he disappeared, his voice could be heard calling back, "*Ja, ja,* Hope Ellison!"

John wrapped his arm around her head, pressing his hand to her hot forehead. "He was a kind fellow, was he not?"

Hope nodded. "He was more than a kind fellow," she whispered. "He was a friend."

"Hope?"

She rubbed her eyes and looked up. John stood before her.

"You had fallen asleep," he smiled.

"Had I?" she asked groggily, lifting her head from the sack of apples.

"Yes. However, perhaps I have a proposal that will cheer you. Joshua and I are heading down to the wharf to glimpse the *Speedwell* once more before we settle down for the night. How would you like to join us?"

Hope shrugged. "If you wish me to," she sighed, frowning as she brushed her skirt, attempting to rid it of the grime that clung to it.

John watched her a moment and seemed about to speak. However, he must have changed his mind, for after a moment of hesitation he merely grinned and led the way across the crowded dock. The modest congregation had chosen it for the night, for it was a lonely one, separated from the rowdy port further up.

It was a short walk to the wharf where the ship was docked, but John and Joshua, who always managed to make simple things lively, kept up an engaging conversation that so amused Hope she entirely forgot about her woes for a moment. Suddenly, John stopped. "There she is," he said softly. "There is the *Speedwell*."

It stood like a mere dark shadow in the twilight's dim light. The silhouette rose before them, the masts reaching out to touch the stars dangling in the sky above. The peaked moon shone palely on its crude outline, illuminating various portions of the ship in a somewhat ghastly way.

However large it seemed against the darkening sky, the *Speedwell* was plainly distinguished from other such ships in the wharf. Hope voiced the difference by stating with all frankness, "'Tis small."

The boys chuckled: a cheerful, honest chuckle, but it was shaded with the soft regret that whispered in their minds, for they were boys after all, and the wild beauty of tall sailing ships was firmly implanted in their masculine minds.

"'Twas the best we could get for a small price," John said. "A small price will buy you but a small ship."

"Yes," Joshua said grimly. "But much freedom costs much regarding price, and that is my chief concern."

Hope glanced at him sharply.

"Cheer up, old chap!" John exclaimed, slapping his friend on the back. "My heart is in the venture, and I have faith we will succeed."

Joshua rubbed his chin. "Yes," he said slowly. "My faith is alongside yours as well. My only concern is how high the price will be."

A chill tingled down Hope's spine, and she instinctively edged closer to John.

"Joshua, we will emerge victorious," John said quietly, as he slipped an arm around Hope's shoulders. "I know we will."

"Catch!"

John tossed Hope an apple. She shot him a flash of a smile as she grabbed it, but even as she fingered the firm red fruit her stomach flopped.

"Catch," she said with a small smile as she tossed it back.

"Hope," John said seriously, "we shall not see fresh fruit like this for a long while."

"Exactly!" Hope cried. "That is why my stomach does not feel right."

John glanced at her. "Very well," he replied, slipping it in his pocket.

Hope squirmed as she watched the crowd around her. The fire flickered on each sober face and caused a few shed tears to glisten. The preacher knelt in the middle of the circle and began to pour out a fervent prayer that sounded frighteningly high-pitched and menacing in the darkness around them. The water lapped just a few yards away, and Hope dared not gaze out at the lonely horizon; yet that did not keep the loneliness from reaching her. It snuck in through the cracks of the tight circle and foamed up like a mist. It sucked the coziness out of the flickering fire, seemingly turning it pale and listless. The prayers that were uttered sounded hollow, and even the arm John slipped around her shoulders seemed insecure among the frightening loneliness that threatened to take over entirely.

The assured feeling she once had, she realized, was now slipping away. Nothing felt it would last. This awful reality haunted her throughout the night and left everything feeling blank and numb and oddly surreal though she knew it weren't a dream.

Morning came sooner than Hope had wished, but it was also a relief after the weight of the night. No one had slept, but that was little matter. 'Twas the stress causing the dark circles under the eyes, not the sleeplessness.

With dread, Hope gazed up at the ship that rose

immense before her eyes, illuminated by the morning light. Supposedly it was home for a few months; yet her heart wrenched at the thought, and she refused to ever consider it home. Holland was her home.

It was a troop of sad voyagers that boarded the ship. Hope clutched John's hand with a tight grip and shivered at the breeze. Her gaze followed the foreboding mast that rose up until it seemed to touch the sun and disappear into a ball of fire that burned her eyes. She blinked and shook her head fiercely.

Her only comfort was that, perhaps, this was merely a dream. She should wake up soon, and she tried to settle on this thought comfortably. However, deep down she knew this was real, and that reality she couldn't shake off, no matter how hard she tried.

The time of parting had come. Pastor Robinson fell down on the deck, tears streaming down his face and soaking his dark beard. Lifting up hands that shook uncontrollably, he sent a prayerful cry up toward the heavens that was filled with such a woeful mourning Hope's heart trembled with sobs. Her throat tightened up until she could scarcely breathe unless she let the tears flow.

Burying her face in her hands, she let them leak through her dry eyelids, gently at first; yet soon they came in torrents. Her body shook and loud wails escaped her lips. Try as she might, she couldn't compose herself. It was now that it felt like reality. It wasn't a mere feeling of reality; it *was* reality. And it hit her so harshly it stole her breath away and left her with a miserable amount of hopeless wailing.

She barely noticed John cuddle her up in his arms or the sobs of her fellow voyagers. Her thoughts swirled is if in a whirlwind, and none would focus long enough to distinguish itself.

Only one thought crossed her head that stayed long enough to be discerned: this must be misery.

Holland is *out there. 'Twasn't just a dream.* Hope gazed woefully at the place her homeland would stand had the horizon not gotten in the way.

"Are you still standing there?" the scornful voice scalded Hope's heart. "You have been there since we left shore."

Hope whirled around. Patience Danford stood behind her, a look of contempt in her dark eyes. The freckles on her nose stood out against her pale skin, and the wind whipped her red curls around her slight face. She squinted pointedly at Hope, and Hope knew she was reminding her that she could see she had been sobbing. Her face blazed red as she knew Patience would not forget this scene and would perhaps one day use it to humiliate her. Now the girl placed her hands on her hips disdainfully, saying, "You shall come down to the hold with me."

"Oh, I shall, shall I?" Hope returned sharply.

"Yes," Patience replied shrilly, "you shall."

"And why is it you are so sure?" Hope crossed her arms and scowled darkly at the slight girl.

"Your mother wishes you to do so."

This haughty comment sent Hope in a tremble of fury; why had she not said so at first?

"She sent me to fetch you."

Hope opened her mouth to send back a stinging

remark, but at that precise moment a gust of wind came swirling across the deck, hitting Patience straight on in such a manner Hope wondered if it was God sent. This being, she thought it only right to smirk at Patience's clumsiness, and she did so, gazing with severity into Patience's dark eyes.

"Oh!" was the first exclamation that escaped Patience's lips, and it hinted at a sob; yet suddenly she regained her haughty position. However, she must not have been able to think of a word to say, or perhaps she grew afraid when she saw the contempt in Hope's eyes. She merely shot her a glare before flouncing away, stumbling now and again as she made her way across the rocking deck.

With an exasperated sigh, Hope twisted to gaze at the empty space on the ocean before turning to follow after Patience to the 'tween deck. This simple act, however, turned into more of a feat that required talent, for Hope had not grown accustomed to the rocking of the ship as it sailed across the choppy waters.

The sails snapped overhead as she slowly inched her way across the deck, her arms flailed out in attempt to control her balance. Her head began to spin as she glanced at the ever-moving waters, and when she looked back at the firm deck, it seemed to swim before her eyes. She couldn't regain a firm landing anywhere.

She became vaguely aware of a hoot of laughter as a rough sailor pushed past, but that seemed to merge together after a moment with visions of rolling waters and unsteady decks. Her stomach began to turn over sourly, but she barely noticed as she struggled to keep reality before her.

Suddenly a movement across the deck caught her attention, and with a leap of hope she wondered if she saw

John crossing the deck. Then she didn't; then she did again, and with utter relief she realized it was true. She stretched out her arms like she did when she was a little girl, and to her relief he lifted her up into his without question.

Resting her weary head on his shoulder, she wondered vaguely if she should be embarrassed of her appearance. She was sure Patience would smirk. Nevertheless, she felt she could deal with that later, and she snuggled up on John's shoulder. Very soon, she was carried off to a land of darkness, where one could know nothing and feel nothing: a pleasant respite from her current troubles.

Cry of Hope

CHAPTER V
Wanderers With a Purpose

"There England stands." John pointed to the green strip of land that stood out distinctly against the horizon.

Hope leaned against the railing as the ocean breeze whipped her sleep-trodden hair around her sweaty cheeks. A smile flickered across her face. "Shall we reach there by nightfall?"

John grinned. "I should hope so, but it never hurts to leave room for unwonted events. A gale could sweep in, perhaps. Sea life is always full of uncertainty."

The sleep had refreshed Hope, and a smile softly crossed her face; she leaned her chin on her fist, grateful for a lull in the turbulent life she seemed to behold. Her eyes darted across the sight ahead of her. White sails dotted the glistening ocean surface, bright and pure in the sunlight. Somewhere among the crowd the *Mayflower* was docked, waiting to join their lonely little ship on the voyage to America.

The rocking deck beneath her feet still felt odd, she

noticed with a slight smile; yet she felt that she had already grown more accustomed to it. Her heart warmed when John said, "Hope, you and I must have saltwater in our blood. Why, sea life seems to agree with us as violently as it disagrees with others. I feel livelier upon the deck of the ship already!"

Hope grinned. "Perchance our destiny is sailing," she said sprightly.

John shook his head, suddenly growing sober. "No. Our destiny is settling in an unknown land in hopes of emerging free from the physical bondage of this world. We are wanderers, in a sense, searching for a land that echoes with the wide expanse of freedom it offers that allows us to worship God unashamedly. Sailors we aren't; pilgrims we are."

Hope gazed at him as he spoke, looking into his calm eyes as fear rose in her throat. "But suppose we don't find that free land?" she asked, her voice rising. "Suppose 'tis not what we expect? Suppose... suppose our hopes turn to dust?"

John's eyes darted to her face, which was frozen in a position that indicated discouragement but quavered on the brink of terror. "Hope," he said softly, tilting his head toward her. "As long as we have faith, hope can never die."

Hope dared look up into his brown eyes, soft in the late afternoon light. She opened her mouth to speak, but no sound came out; she realized she had nothing to say. Her mind swam, refusing to stand still despite Hope's longing to gather her queer feelings into steady thoughts.

She turned abruptly, leaning her elbows on the railing and looking down into the water lapping against the side of the ship. It sung a song of the wild intrigue and adventure of sailing—sailing to unknown lands, sailing to unknown horizons, sailing to unknown fates and futures. Hope shivered.

Pilgrims we are. Longing tore at her throat as she wondered if she would ever have the confidence that surrounded John, and she edged closer to her brother, who seemed to be a steady rock despite her unsteady ground.

He instinctively slipped an arm around her shoulders and looked down at the dark head below his shoulder. The matted hair was tangled and dirty, but he looked tenderly at it as if it were the most precious thing aboard. Hope heard his voice murmur above her, "If our faith is unbreakable, our hopes will never leave us. Oh, Hope, please never forget it."

The words locked in Hope's head, and though she would forget them at intervals in the future, they would return at the most opportune timings: that tender voice just above her head whispering softly words of wisdom expressed by one with knowledge well beyond his years.

The hustle and bustle of the crowd below fascinated Hope to no end. She perched on the rail of the ship, clutching it with white knuckles as she observed with curiosity the interesting scenes that went on at rapid pace. She witnessed a woman losing her three children, and she took part in the recovery by shouting out gaily the whereabouts of the poor lady's brood from her view on the tall ship. She silenced three obnoxious boys who shouted "puritan" with one swift expression that must have curdled milk, and she constantly had one eye kept on an enormous black hog that went snuffling through the crowd for hours. Wherever that old hog went, delightful trouble of all kinds followed. She choked with laughter when he upset a red-faced peddler's wares: a cart full of sticky fruits that went rolling and tumbling through the tumultuous crowd, becoming squashed by some running boot or splattering on a pompous girl's petticoats, causing Hope to chuckle so hard she nearly lost her balance on the edge of the ship.

From dawn the day the *Speedwell* docked, to dusk when Mother called her down to meal, she sat watching the activity of Southampton, England, all the while marveling at how dry a country the land was. The cobbled stone streets were dusty compared to Holland's neat sidewalks, and she gaped in wonder at the utter solidness of the roads themselves. No glittering canal soaked up the evening light. Barges seemed to be banned from existence, and as far as the eye could see, water remained hidden from view, though Hope strained her green eyes desperately for a glimpse of the familiar combination of earth and water that so reminded her of her homeland. But neither seemed to agree with the other, for water seemed to prefer not entering the land as it stayed safely in it's place under the rocking deck beneath her feet, while the earth seemed to have a distaste for such substances—the only water Hope glimpsed was the soap water and waste dumped carelessly in the ditch by the roadside, causing foul vapors to rise so strongly that it filled the harbor with such a stench Hope could catch whiffs of it when a soft breeze blew.

By mid-afternoon, Hope was startled out of a deep reverie of said matters, when a voice from behind asked calmly, "What do you think?"

She gasped and whirled. "John!" she said indignantly, as she came face-to-face with her brother. "You frightened me!"

John grinned and leaned his elbows on the railing

next to her, his eyes sweeping over the land before him. "It has been a long time since I saw this country last," he said wistfully.

Hope paused. Her eyes swept the scene before her once again. The lined streets, the dusty roads, the everlasting stench, and the bustling crowd all filled her mind in a swift glance. Her eyebrows knitted together as she wondered how her brother could think so fondly of a country that seemed to possess little beauty compared to beloved Holland.

"What do you think of it?" John asked again.

Hope squirmed. "'Tisn't Holland," she muttered.

John grinned and tousled her hair, shaking off the wistful mood. "Might I presume you prefer what you consider your homeland to mine?"

Hope glanced at him as a half-smile trembled at her lips. "I prefer beauty," she said honestly but sharply, "and I haven't seen such things in this land as of yet."

"Ah. And what might you mean by beauty?"

"Oh, the canals, the gardens, the sidewalks, the windmills…" Hope's voice trailed off as a lump began to gnaw at her throat. "'Tis my homeland,"—her voice grew hard—"'twill never be another."

John was silent. His eyes darted toward Hope. After a long moment, he said, "Hope, look at the horizon."

She glanced behind her. There it lay, sharply defined in the dusky light, for the sun was setting from the opposite side, casting it's illuminative rays upon the intricate line that separated the sea from the sky far off in the distance. "I see it," she said softly. "Holland stands just beyond it."

"Yes, Hope," John said quietly, but an unusual sharpness pierced the gentle tone. "Holland lies there. Now look at the hill beyond Southampton."

Hope did so without murmur, but her stomach twisted with a mixture of indignation and heat. She crossed her arms over her chest in half-fear, waiting to see what her brother would say next.

"Another horizon lies beyond that hill. Only that horizon holds the future, while the horizon you so love to look at holds the past." John paused, and Hope glanced at him with green eyes that wavered between severity and pain. "Hope, which are you going to set your heart on?"

Hope glanced up into his brown eyes, then quickly looked away from his penetrating gaze. She tried to shrug off his question, but it seemed to remain pinned in the air, unanswered and unspoken of, but still heavily present for a long while afterward.

Cry of Hope

CHAPTER VI
Days of Old

"This is a meal?"

The incredulous remark escaped Hope's lips almost before she realized it, and her cheeks burnt red as she caught the disapproving glances cast her direction. Joshua jabbed her in the ribs with his elbow from the right side of her, and John hissed from the left, "Hope, watch your tongue!"

The dinner had been served that evening, and it appeared their portions were less than usual. Hope's growling stomach didn't take too well to the change, and her accidental remark had slipped out before she had a chance to reckon with it.

She glanced down at her trencher. Hardtack, a slice of cheese, and a pewter mug filled only halfway with beer—Hope felt it could scarcely be considered a meal at all. Gingerly she reached down and picked up the hardtack. She fingered it distastefully for a moment before dropping the victual back on the trencher with a resounding clack: a noise, Hope privately thought, that should be saved for coins or pebbles or knitting needles, *not* something that was meant to be consumed.

"Must I eat it?" Hope whispered to John pleadingly.

"Be grateful for your food, Hope," her brother said softly, "for we may run short before the trip is over."

Hope's stomach lurched. "Why do we not simply buy enough provisions for the trip?" she whimpered, her eyes wide.

"Short funds," Joshua muttered from the other side of her. "'Tisn't the easiest matter finding work here in England. One would think our homeland would be slightly more friendly to our coming," he said with a mixture of bitterness and indignation.

Hope glanced at John. He clenched his jaw and stared at the cheese in his hand with a hard expression on his face. "Yes," he said, his tone soft. "It seems our country has always been against us in some way or another."

Hope's eyes softened as she looked into his face; it showed no trace of bitterness, but rather a sober sadness over his homeland. "How has it always been against us?" she asked and shifted closer to him.

He glanced at her. "I suppose you have only heard it a few times," he murmured, setting the cheese down on his trencher. "Might as well tell you once again."

Joshua leaned in to hear the account, and so John began. "We lived in a small village called Scrooby about twelve years back. You were a mere baby, Hope, and I was but a little child of four. Father was a blacksmith, but the funds were low, so Mother ran a shop for baked delicacies—cakes and tarts and such—to bring in extra wages. My, was she but a strong woman, caring for two children and a bakery shop at the same time!

Cry of Hope

"Our little congregation was small still then. We met in secret by night, for the orders given by King James of England remained firm under the law that every citizen and inhabitant of the land were to attend his pompous church whether he wished to or not. You see, because of this, were we to reject his church, we were traitors to his rule and to the English government as well.

"Our congregation banded together during this time, and we all stayed firm to our convictions and kept away from such churches, despite the rule of King James. Every other night Father would lock the door to the shop, and we all would slip out the back, Mother carrying you in her arms and I holding fast to Father's hand. Near the same time several of our neighbors would be slipping out in the same manner, and all would head, one by one, toward Elder Brewster's inn, our most common place for meeting to worship God in secret.

"All went well for a while, but soon we began to realize that we could not remain meeting in secrecy for long. King James would find out we were not attending his church. He would find out, send his soldiers, and throw the men into prison, leaving the women and children helpless.

"Several serious discussions followed these fears. You see, were we torn apart and persecuted, it would do not one of us good. There seemed only one way out of these perils—escape.

"Our first attempt began shortly after this conclusion was made. Holland seemed the only logical destination, for it was the only country not under bondage. Father sold our shop to a lone traveler, who wished to settle down in a little town and take up a business. We stayed in Elder Brewster's inn until his was sold, and around that time most of us were ready to set sail. We had hired a small ship to take us to Holland, and we made plans to meet down at a lonely beach by night.

"We waited for many hours, often wondering if it would ever come. When finally it did, the men hurriedly loaded the ship; the women and children boarded it last. We breathed a sigh of relief when all were safely on board. No soldiers had been spotted, and we would be well on our way before they knew we were gone."

John trailed off. He looked down at his hands, saying nothing, until Joshua continued, a grim but steady expression of face. "John and I were but small children at the time, Hope, though good friends nevertheless. We strayed from our mothers when our congregation encircled in prayer. Curiosity had overcome the two of us, and we began to roam the ship but a few short minutes after we had boarded. I remember slowly opening a heavy door and stepping inside. I ran headlong into a tall man. One glance upward, and I saw a frightening pointed nose glaring down at me. A horrid smile crossed the man's red cheeks when he noticed my pale face, and with a crack of his cane, he brought down a searing mark across my back. I wanted to run and tell Father of the intruder on board, but the pain was so great..." Joshua paused and swallowed. He clenched his fists with a hard look across his face and muttered, "That general was cruelty itself."

John cleared his throat and began speaking. "With a whip of his cane, he had pushed me into Joshua, who was writhing in pain. I cried out to Father that soldiers were aboard, but my warning did little good, for they had surrounded our poor congregation already. They were all going to prison. I was terrified of being left behind, so I dragged Joshua to the middle of the circle. His mother broke into tears when she saw the pain he was in, and I daresay his father would have gotten revenge on the general had he not been clapped in irons."

Hope sat, one hand flung involuntarily across her lips. Never in her life had she heard such a detailed account of their flight from England. Pensive silence fell for a moment until she asked in a hushed whisper, "How then did we escape?"

Joshua glanced at her. "We were penniless. The captain of the ship, who had made a deal with the king, had taken our money. We had sold nearly everything we owned, and what we had left, the soldiers took. It seemed a hopeless situation, I daresay. Yet, we did not give up. The women and children were released from the dismal prisons first, and later the men. We began planning another escape.

"But, Hope, the men were watched carefully from then on. It was crucial to plot a strategic escape. It was decided that the women and children should be sent down a stream ahead of the men on a raft, while they instead took a ship down the river. We intended on meeting up again as the two merged together.

"The night we parted was frightening. We did not know whether we would see one another again. I remember... I remember my father taking me aside, embracing me and telling me to be good to Mother. I did not understand it at the time, yet now I see he was preparing me to take his place in the future, if we never saw him again in this world." Joshua paused, his eyes glistening with fervor in the golden light.

John took up the recount then, saying, "Our plan seemed secure. Yet still we had troubles. The women and children reached the end of the stream first. It was windy, cold, and several of us were terribly seasick, so we slipped close to the shore, where the water was calmer. But the raft became caught in a muddy dune. We were helpless. We could only hope that the ship would come soon.

"But then the soldiers came. I remember sitting near Mother as she held you, as the sun rose early in the morning. She was singing softly to you, Hope, when of a sudden there were swarms of armed soldiers around us. We were caught—arrested once again. It was as a rough soldier grabbed me firmly in his arms that I saw over his shoulder the ship passing through—and Father's face watching me from one of the portholes. I nearly shrieked to him when I clapped my hand over my mouth, remembering the secrecy of our plans. Instead, I haplessly watched the ship go by, for the captain was heartless enough to refuse the men's bidding to come to us.

"Now we were penniless again, and worse, Father was in Holland. By grace, he found work there and managed to sent money back to help with the funds needed to hire another ship."

"After all of the struggles to escape England's tyranny," finished Joshua, "we finally were safe together in Holland. Now here we are sailing to Northern Virginia, again journeying to an unknown land for the sake of our freedoms."

Hope was silent for a moment. "After all of the troubles in England," she said, "you still wish to consider it your homeland?" She looked at them both sharply. "Why so?"

John took a deep breath and looked at her. "I consider it my homeland because it is my homeland. There is no way to sidle by that fact, and there is no way I would wish to. The cultural essence of the dear land only seems marred because of the evil a few men wished to bestow on us, and I shan't let them diminish my opinion of that culture however much they try to with their crude ways and sharp tongues. They may crush us in body, but they cannot crush us in spirit, and as long I may live I will not let them stamp out my pride for such a familiar and dear background that has kept me safely an outsider to Holland and will be the root for the civilization of our settlement in Northern Virginia."

    Hope glanced at Joshua. He sat, leaning his chin on his fists. Looking up with something like hard determination glistening to the very corners of his hazel eyes, he nodded. "Yes," said he quietly, "I as well."

CHAPTER VII
Confliction

"Come, Hope!" a voice cried cheerfully. "Let us go down to the garden and stroll! Or perhaps you would rather walk along the dike?"

Hope whirled and blinked her eyes in surprise. Constance? Her face broke into a grin, and she squealed, "Constance!"

"Why, what is wrong?"

"I thought we had left you in Holland!"

"You did."

"But you are here!"

"And so are you."

After a moment of stunned silence, Hope laughed and linked arms with her friend. Together they ran on light feet. Hope could hardly believe the good fortune that was suddenly bestowed upon her, and she began running all the faster in glee. "Come, Constance, let us run harder!" she cried.

"No, no, Hope, I cannot run that fast!"

"Run, Constance, run!"

Cry of Hope

"I cannot, Hope, I cannot." The words faded as her friend fell behind. Desperately, Hope tried to slow, but some unperceivable force kept her feet running, running, running. She gasped and tried to wrench her head around, but it seemed stuck fast to her shoulders, neither turning nor twisting in any way. Her eyelids felt heavy, and suddenly she saw a blue expanse stretching before her. The firm sidewalk had disappeared from underneath her feet, and she was flying. Flying faster and faster, away from Holland and away from Constance, leaving them both miles and miles behind.

Hope started. Reaching up with trembling hands, she wiped away the hot tears that flowed down her face. Her heart tore as she realized she had been dreaming. Rubbing her eyes, she muttered determinedly, "Holland is my homeland. Never will it be another."

"Hope!" a voice cried urgently.

She froze.

"Hope!" the voice said again, and this time she sat up. Now she realized it was John calling her. She stood, stumbling a little as the ship tilted beneath her feet and cringing as she rubbed her stiff back uncomfortably. "Yes?" she asked and stumbled again as the ship gave a lurch. *This is queer*, she thought, *the ship has not tilted this way in over a week. Not since we were sailing to—*

She gasped. "Have we set sail for the New World?" she cried.

John emerged from the shadows with a laugh. "Yes, Hope," he grinned, "we set sail nearly twenty minutes ago. England is still in sight if you would like to take one last look at her."

Hope wiped her eyes and nodded. The next moment

she was leaning against the railing of the ship—an act she had quickly grown accustomed to—gazing out for the last time at the land upon which she had been born.

"I suppose this our last time seeing England," she murmured, glancing at her brother. He gave a slight nod, never taking his eyes off of his homeland. His brown eyes looked sad with regret, and Hope realized with a tear at her throat that her brother could perhaps relate more to her than she had thought. She looked back at the strip of land that stretched out on both sides and leaned her head against John's arm.

He grinned and seemed to shake off his dejected feelings quickly, saying with a short laugh, "Care for a run around the deck?" He was off in a heartbeat, and Hope giggled, following suit.

The rocking deck still felt queer beneath their feet and occasionally they would skid or stumble; but they were up again in an instant, laughing as if they were having the time of their lives. John leapt over crates and coils of rope as Hope chased after him recklessly, exclaiming, "John Ellison, how unfair!" She didn't seem to think it terribly unfair, however, for while she was exclaiming she was giggling hysterically all the while.

Their infectious game brought Joshua to join in, and oh! what a rowdy, delightful time they had! A stumble upon deck would slow them down for an instant, but then another would pass by with a cheerful taunt that caused them to jump to their feet and chase after the other with a giggle or a shout that kept them in their best spirits. For a long while the game kept on until Hope collapsed against a barrel, stuttering between gasps and giggles that she was worn out. John and

Joshua stopped as well, knowing the game wouldn't hold the same amusement without the spunky girl to keep them on their toes, and therefore sat to rest next to her. It was as they were lounging in the sun that Hope and Patience had their first serious clash.

Patience had strolled on the deck amidst the middle of the game, but none had noticed her through their own cheerful tumult. So she stood, half hidden by a large barrel, watching their rowdy play with her arms crossed over her chest, and her brow furrowed.

When Hope sat down, her sharp eyes caught Patience's billow of curly red hair blowing in the breeze. Patience's eyes met with Hope's at the same moment, and she stepped from her spot with her chin lifted in a way that hinted at defiance. A spark shot in Hope's chest, but she kept outwardly calm, watching Patience sharply. She walked nonchalantly across the deck, but she seemed to be watching Hope and the boys out of the corner of her eye. Suddenly she turned toward them. "Hallo, Hope," she said warily.

"Hallo," Hope replied coldly.

Patience reached up and touched her red curls. "Rather windy?"

"Some."

"Troubling, is it not?"

"Not particularly. Why then did you come on deck, if the breeze troubles you so much?" Hope asked, her tone calm, though her expression remained challenging.

"Oh, the hold felt rather dank," Patience replied, her hand clutching her red hair with a fierce grip.

"Was it?" Hope asked, sarcasm stinging her tone. "What a surprise."

Patience narrowed her dark eyes sharply, and Hope returned the favor undaunted. Then Patience asked a dangerous question. "Sorrowful about leaving Holland, eh?"

Hope snapped out of her leisurely seat in a second, her hands ripping down to her sides. "You do not know when to stay in your place, do you, Patience Danford?" she seethed.

Patience looked taken aback, but she kept her stand, saying with a hazardous look in her eye, "*I* do not know my place? How humorous. Were you not the one who impetuously demanded our own pastor to reveal to you where his niece was?" Hope's eyes glazed over with fiery temper, but Patience kept on. "Were you not the one who returned to the barge only after your brother dragged you?" The hands hanging stiff at Hope's sides began to curl into clenched fists. "And all because you dared not say farewell to a friend you might never see in this world again." Patience grasped a red curl and stared at Hope with stony eyes.

"Patience Danford, you jackanapes!" the words ripped out of Hope's mouth. "You are a bitter, uncaring child, Patience, who would not know love from hatred!" she spat, finding with shock how easily they flowed.

Patience's face turned pale, and she took a step back. "*I* do not know love?" she croaked, her face tight. "'Tis *you* who knows not love, Hope Ellison."

Hope glowered and might have lunged at the girl had John not suddenly put a firm hand on Hope's shoulder. "Let us go down to the hold now, Hope," he said quietly, turning her toward the ladder. She followed without struggle, but halfway across the deck she glanced back at Patience. She stood near the rail, her arms crossed over her chest. Her red curls blew wildly in the breeze, and she was staring down at the deck beneath her feet. Glancing up, she saw Hope watching her, and with a glare, she turned and flounced away. Hope trembled in fury, but let John firmly lead her below deck to keep her out of another collision with Patience Danford for a while.

"John," Hope asked that evening, her hair mussed and her heart thumping as she hurried toward him. "Is it true?"

"Is what true?" he asked carelessly, looking up from the piece of wood he was whittling.

"Was the *Speedwell* leaking?"

The absent-minded look flew from John's eyes. He glanced up sharply, asking quietly, "Who told you so?"

Hope's knees grew shaky, and she sat down in a heap next to him. "Then it *is* true?" she asked anxiously.

John sighed and set the wood and knife down. He leaned his elbows on his knees, rubbing his chin. "Yes, Hope." He looked at her. "'Tis true."

"But *why*?" she cried, her throat clamming up. "*Why* was it leaking?"

"The shipbuilders took a look at her, and they said they had patched her up. There must have been holes in the structure: punctured seams, splintered wood, or perchance damage to the sides. I do not know first-hand, Hope. I never saw the damage. But there *was* a leaking ship, of that I am sure."

Hope was silent, watching his face for any signs of alarm. None came, however, and a peacefulness seemed to have settled over it. "So there is no danger?" she pressed.

"The shipbuilders have assured us she is fit for the voyage."

Hope breathed a sigh of relief, though something like uneasiness tickled in her mind. *The shipbuilders declare 'tis safe*, she said to herself, shrugging off the haunting sensation, *and the shipbuilders* must *be right.*

Cry of Hope

CHAPTER VIII
Sea Troubles

"Hope!"

The voice seemed miles away from her sleepy presence. She rolled over, pulling the rough coverlet over her ears.

"Hope!"

It rang again, louder this time. She felt a pain bite her elbow, and she yelped, wriggling away.

"Hope!"

Suddenly her mind came to life in a shock, and she leapt, her eyelids flying open and her hair a tangled muss. "What is it?" she gasped. "Oh, what is it?"

"Hope!" Mother leaned over her, pinching her elbow tightly. Her face was illuminated by the dim lantern light, looking paler than usual, and she wore an anxious expression that caused Hope's stomach to squeeze in fear.

"What is it, Mother?" she whimpered.

"The *Speedwell* appears to be leaking once again. Father says we must go upon deck. The men have begun working at the pumps, and the sailors are steering her toward land, but we must be prepared for the anything that may happen." The words came out in one breath, yet those few words seemed to relay a hundred fears into Hope's head. *The Speedwell was leaking.* Her face paled, and she bit her lip tightly as Mother wrapped her arm around Hope's shoulder and ushered her toward the ladder.

Her frozen expression burst into a cry, however, when she caught sight of John, pumping away with all of his might in the corner. Mother tugged on her arm, but Hope ripped away and ran over to John, flinging her arms around his neck.

"Now, now, Hope," he said softly in response to her whimper, pausing his work for only a moment. "Go on deck, there's a good girl. I will be up presently to bring you news of the progress. Do not cry, 'twill be alright. Now, *go.*" And giving her a gentle push, John returned to his grinding work. Hope turned and scrambled up the ladder.

As she emerged on deck, the stickiness of the hold fell away, and a soothing ocean breeze blew her matted hair back from her cheeks. Her ruffled spirits calmed greatly, and she tilted her head back, soaking in the awesome sight that suddenly washed before her eyes. The sky seemed to have transformed, as if a multitude of glittering diamonds had gathered together to turn the normal fathomless black pool to a rich dark blue ocean. Her mouth fell open in wonder, and she breathed outwardly the sigh of an awestruck onlooker. "Remarkable," she whispered.

"Hope!" Her mother's call interrupted her moment of amazement, and she, for once, obeyed immediately.

The women and children sat gathered together near the forecastle that appeared to offer some protection from the night air. A metal brazier had been set up in the middle of the circle, and a flame danced inside among the coals, flickering across the anxious faces of those settled around it.

Hope slipped in amongst the crowd. Folding her legs under her skirt, she leaned her back against a barrel. However, she didn't stay put long, for the lapping of the water called her to the ship's rail. There the night was quieter, except for a wisp of murmurs coming from the circle of housewives.

Hope's eyes scanned the horizon, and she shivered. 'Twas dark, and only a mere line traced where the ocean met the sky far off. She squinted, trying to see any sign of life or light, but none appeared; she dropped her eyes to the water directly below. It lapped against the ship, seeming to jeer the boat with a taunting laugh—a reminder that *it* could swallow the ship with little force, *it* had the power to overcome such a tiny vessel.

Suddenly, Hope noticed a pale light reflecting off the water, growing brighter and brighter until the moon burst forth from behind a shielding cloud, shining across the lonely waters and soaking up some of the frightening darkness that lurked about.

"*Now* 'tis beautiful!" Hope whispered to herself, as her eyes swept the palely-tinted waters that danced in the enchanting moonlight.

"Ah, but you will not think it so beautiful when this rotting ship sinks and sends us into those choppy waters," a voice said with eerie melancholy behind her.

Hope whirled and came face-to-face with Patience Danford, who stood just behind her, hugging her chest with a chilled look on her face.

"Oh, *must* you ruin peaceful moments?" Hope said in

almost a whine.

"I was not doing anything of the sort," Patience said sorely. "I was simply stating the obvious facts that must be running through the heads of every passenger aboard."

"Perchance some passengers prefer to look on the bright side of things."

"*Is* there a bright side?" Patience's question caught Hope off guard. "Hope, whether you realize it or not, this ship *is* leaking, and we could be caught in that cold, cold ocean in but a few hours. We could die, Hope. We could *drown* in those murky waters." There was a catch in Patience's voice, but she turned quickly and flounced into the shadows, away from Hope's view.

Hope's lips closed in a tight line, and she leaned over the railing fuming for a moment. Her finger ran along a splinter in the rail, tracing its rough, crooked line. She leaned back and gazed up at the stars, twinkling and sparkling, unfazed by the harsh conversation she had just had with Patience. *Unchanging still...* Hope sighed and pivoted, slipping back to Mother.

***

A rumble of voices awoke her. She winced, and her hand flew up to her cheek where a cold pain shot through upon her awakening. A barrel, she discovered, was not the softest place to lay one's head. She gazed up at the paling sky. Dawn was coming. She took in a deep breath, breathing in the cool morning air that revived her groggy state of mind. Breezes rippled across her face, creating a dancing pattern that made her grin from its renewing freshness. She leaned her head back, gazing up at the great white sails that snapped in the wind.

Her eyes caught a movement to her left, and her attention immediately turned toward it. John came stumbling up the ladder, his face flushed and his boots soaked. He ran a hand through his dark matted hair and took a deep breath upon reaching the fresh air.

"John!" Hope cried and jumped to her feet.

He managed a grin at her disheveled figure and said wearily, "Hallo, Hope. I made a promise to you that I would bring you news, and so I have. 'Tis leaking as much as before, but we are keeping the water out—as we did before. Nothing seems to have changed—seems quite discouraging." He sat down with a gasp next to her.

She glanced at him anxiously.

John gave a short laugh—a mix between a snort and a gasp—saying, "Yes, Hope, we shall reach Dartmouth in plenty of time. The water is being sent out just as quickly as 'tis coming in. We will be quite safe."

Hope snuggled in next to him. "I suppose the shipbuilders were wrong," she said.

He nodded slowly. "I suppose so."

"I suppose we cannot fully trust what *they* say about the ship any longer?"

John was silent. "Perchance you are right." His brows knitted together in deep thought, and his hand roughly pushed back the dark hair sticking to Hope's forehead.

"John Ellison!" a voice shouted from the ladder to the hold. "Your work is not yet over and idleness pushes your load onto us. Get a move on!"

John grinned at Hope. "Alas, back to the prison I go,

sister. 'Tis a shame being a sixteen-year-old lad on days such as this." He winked at her before heading back down to work, rubbing his sore arms as he did so.

Hope laughed and waved back, but noticed the slack in his usual stride and desperately hoped they would reach Dartmouth soon. The men were growing weary after a full night at the pumps.

Cry of Hope

CHAPTER IX
Rising and Falling Hopes

It was evening. The stars were growing bright in the darkening sky. Hope leaned against the rail, resting her chin on her arm. She closed her eyes, feeling the cool breeze kiss her cheeks. The town of Dartmouth sent up a hum of homey sounds that soothed her unsettled spirits. It felt good to relax.

Suddenly two familiar voices reached her ears, and she stiffened, turning her head in the direction of the sound. Father and John appeared, half-hidden in the growing shadows. John was speaking anxiously. "Father, are you certain the men have come to the right verdict concerning the *Speedwell?*"

"Why should I not?" Father replied sharply. His gray eyes glinted in the light of the moon. Hope felt heat rising in her throat, and she clenched the wooden rail.

John continued, appearing undaunted. "Sir, the other night Hope supposed that we could not trust the word of the shipbuilders any longer, for the *Speedwell* has begun to take on water twice now. I see her reasoning behind it, and it has been on my mind ever since. What cause do we have to believe she will not leak again, I ask?" He ran a hand through his disheveled hair. "Father, do you think she may?"

Father bit his lip before asking gruffly, "What are you suggesting?"

John shifted. "Leave the *Speedwell* behind."

"*What?*" The words ripped out of Father's mouth, cutting sharply into the ears of both John and the unknown listener, who winced and felt tears start to her eyes. "John Ellison," Father said between his teeth, "I have little knowledge of what possessed such a thought to come to your mind. 'Tis too dangerous for a lone ship on the Atlantic, you hear? Far too dangerous!"

"But, Father!" John cried, gripping the rim of a barrel. "'Tis far more dangerous to trust such a clumsy ship to carry us there safely! More dangerous still to waste time on matters that may prove fatal in the first place. Father, the winter winds... they may set in earlier than we expect and hinder our work. What is more, there are women and children aboard. They are frailer than we, and if they are exposed to such fearfully cold elements, they may suffer on account of a wrong decision *we* might make!" He flung his arms into the air, breathing heavily as he looked his father in the eyes.

Father strode forward, grasping his son's shoulders with trembling hands. "John Ellison," he barked. "John Ellison, I will not have you meddling in the business of the elders—no!" He held up his hand as John started to speak, giving him a sharp shake. "A wrong decision, you say?" He grimaced. "'Tis high time you come to reality, John. The world is full of options, and all you can do is come to a verdict and pray for the best. Do you hear me? 'Tis time you toss aside childish ways, and 'tis time you stop coming to conclusions from an offhand comment made by a child of mere thirteen! Wake up! 'tis time you take life as a man!" And with that last bellow, Father turned and stormed down to the hold.

John's face twisted with pain, and he pivoted and made for the rail. He leaned against it, pressing all his weight toward the New World. No words escaped his lips, but soon a hand slipped through the crook of his arm. "Hallo," Hope murmured, rubbing her eyes.

John gave her a half-smile. "Heard it all, did you?"

"No!—well, I suppose, but..." She looked into his face and swallowed. "Are we truly in danger?"

John gave a shake of his dark hair and sighed. "Perchance." He bit his lip. "I do not know, Hope. I... I do not know."

Hope shuddered, and John slipped an arm around her shoulder. "We will get through alright, despite our little knowledge of what the future holds," he said as he tried to insert a cheery tone to his words.

Hope looked up at him, her green eyes pleading. "Promise?" she whispered.

"Promise."

The *Speedwell* and the *Mayflower* set sail the day after John's confrontation with Father, and though Hope's mind was constantly plagued by John's words, the *Speedwell* appeared to be contradicting such fears and sailed peaceably for many days.

Until one night. Hope was awakened by John. How awfully familiar his words were!

"Awaken, Hope."

Her heart stood still. "Is the *Speedwell*—"

"Yes. Hurry now. Mother wishes you on deck, and all of the men and boys are ordered to work at the pumps."

Hope slipped out of her hammock and allowed him to lead her to the ladder. "Wait!" she cried as he turned.

"What is it?" he hissed.

She flung her arms around his neck, her hands shaking. "Will we be alright?"

"Come now, Hope," he whispered, placing her from him and wiping a few tears from her cheeks. "I promised, did I not?"

Hope nodded.

"Then my promise will be kept. Go to Mother now."

Hope gazed at him for a moment and then turned and clamored up the ladder. Upon deck she bit her lip and stiffly walked to Mother. Resisting the urge to fling her arms around her, she slipped down next to her and satisfied herself by leaning on the barrel she was sitting on. The conversation between the women hummed in her ears, but a tension settled over all like a heavy fog, and lighthearted conversation could not blow it away. Hours past by, yet time seemed to have stood still. The darkness still hung thickly over them, and Hope began to feel sure the *Speedwell* would go under before they could arrive back in England. Her fear gnawed at her throat, and the only comforting thought was John's words. "I promise" hung in her head, and eventually her anxious stomach settled down enough for her to drift off to sleep.

Hope shivered. She turned over and then shivered again. Suddenly her hand flew up to her cheek, and she moaned. The cold iron rim of the barrel cut into her skin, and she slowly sat up, clutching her cheek with pain in her eyes. Releasing her hold, she knew there would be a black and blue bruise before the hour was over. She shivered again and realized a chill breeze was blowing off the Atlantic. "Mother?" she muttered groggily, then caught sight of the women grouped together by the rail.

Climbing clumsily to her feet, Hope stumbled over to them, wincing from the stiffness of her knees that sent an aching pain through her legs. She stopped when she reached the rail. Nothing but an expanse of ocean stood before them. "So England is not in sight," she muttered, hugging her chest with fear and cold.

A clatter by the ladder stole everyone's attention. John stood frozen a moment upon reaching deck, but the next he fell on his knees. "John!" the shriek escaped Hope's lips, and the next thing she knew she was by his side. "Are you alright?" she gasped, reaching out a clammy hand to stroke back the lick of dark hair on his forehead.

"Rather," he panted drily, pushing himself up until he leaned against a barrel. His face was smeared with grime, but that compared not to the exhaustion that filled his countenance. "C-can I get you anything?" Hope asked weakly.

"Rest," John replied bluntly. "The workload down there is nearly unbearable." He mopped his forehead with his damp sleeve. "If we must work continuously in such a way until we reach England, I have my doubts I will be able to do so without falling asleep on my feet." He tossed Hope a half-hearted smile, and she giggled, though it had a nervous ring to it.

"Shall we reach England in time?" she asked, as she slipped beside him.

John glanced at her anxious face and whispered fondly, "I promised we would be alright. Is that not enough?"

Hope glanced at him. "Perchance." She cracked a smile, and he tousled her hair.

"My turn to rest, John," a gasp sounded from the ladder, and Joshua was responded by a laugh from Hope and a groan from John. "Give a fellow a chance to catch his breath, comrade," John complained, as Joshua sat against a barrel across from the two siblings.

"I have," Joshua grinned. "Elder Brewster declared five minutes each man. You have had your share, and mine comes next. Down to the workload you go, John Ellison. Once every other man has had his turn, yours will come around again. 'Tis the way it goes, you know."

"We know." John pushed himself up with a groan. He started down the ladder, but his head popped up again a moment later. "I will let you know, Hope, when I fall asleep on my feet," he said.

Hope laughed and turned back to Joshua. She noticed the marked colour change in his face since the night before, and she bit her lip. He seemed to be soaking in the few minutes of rest he could get, and Hope felt it her duty to leave him at peace. She slipped away as he reclined, finding a secluded place where no one would trouble her. Leaning against the splintered rail, she rested her chin on her fist. The breeze washed over her face and chilled her spine, relieving her hot cheeks. Her mind flew to the men, who slaved at the pumps below. *Oh, for Plymouth to come sooner!* She closed her eyes, breathing in the salty air. Her heart thumped against her chest. *If only Father had listened to John's word,* she though bitterly, *they may not be working so painfully below.* And with that last thought, her mind drifted as if in a daze, wondering and remembering and dreaming of her pleasant days in Holland.

"Plymouth in sight!"

The shout came an entire day later. Cheers erupted on deck, and Hope flung her mob cap into the air. She ran to the opening of the hold, calling out the joyous news to the utterly exhausted workers squeezing out their last bits of strength on the pumps. "Huzzah!" she heard Joshua shout hoarsely, and an incoherent bellow came from John. She smiled but shuddered as well, for the haggard voices sounded on the verge of death itself.

In but another short hour the ship had docked. The shipbuilders arrived shortly, bearing the same news that had been heard one too many times before. "How foolish they would be," Hope muttered to herself, "if they chose to repair her again and continue on."

John emerged on deck soon after and looked ready to drop dead upon a second's notice. He leaned against a barrel and closed his eyes, and Hope knew he was asleep a few moments later. Joshua followed suit, and Hope went to sit between them, her knees hugged to her chest. For several hours the two exhausted boys slept, and Hope found herself growing drowsy as well. She was on the verge of nodding off when John's voice asked softly, "Tired, Hope?"

She turned and saw him looking up at her from his relaxed state, and she smiled. "Perchance. Just looking at the two of you could well make one tired."

"Two sleepless days and nights spent slaving could make any man tired." He smiled at her, sitting up.

She snuggled closer to him, asking, "What decision do you suppose the men will come to this time?"

John shifted. "They would be fools to trust the ship once again," he said bitterly.

Hope nodded. "Yes, but would Father suggest leaving the *Speedwell* behind after his..." Her voice trailed off.

"No," John replied, looking at her. "That is why I hope someone else will mention it. They *must* mention it." He lifted a fist and let it fall back on deck again.

"If they *do* decide to sail the *Speedwell* again," Hope said impishly, "you and I must jump off the side and swim for shore, for there is no way I am sailing on this clumsy vessel any longer."

"'Tis a deal, little sister," John grinned, and they shook on it to seal the pact.

※

"Well, Hope," John said as he approached her a few hours later. "As it so happens, I have been informed that the men have indeed agreed that the *Speedwell* is unreliable, and therefore they are selling her."

"Huzzah!" Hope flung her mob cap into the air for the second time that day. "To whom are they selling her?"

"The very crew of the ship." John smiled.

"Rather convenient."

"Indeed," he replied. "The heated discussion taking place at the moment, however, is on whom will sail on the *Mayflower* and whom will stay behind."

Hope froze. "Stay behind?" she inquired as a strange anticipation arose in her throat. "How do you mean?"

"The *Mayflower* will not hold all who intended on sailing, and therefore some must remain here in England or else sail back to Holland on returning ships," John explained, though a knowing look shone in his eyes, and his face seemed to behold a warning expression.

Holland! Hope's heart leapt until she thought it may be soaring for the first time in many weeks. She began to tremble with excitement. "Do you really mean return to Holland?" she cried.

"Hope." John held up his hand as he leaned against a barrel. "Listen to me for a moment, please? Father is not one to give up so easily." He looked at her eager face before saying slowly, "However, he did appear to dislike the idea of sailing on one meager ship across the entire ocean and therefore *may* decide to stay behind. 'Tis not an easy decision, however, and I would not suggest getting hopes up too high for something that may not happen."

"But John!" Hope's eyes were bright. "How can I help it? 'Tis something I never even dared think might happen!"

"Then do not dare think again," was John's warning reply. He looked at her a moment before saying softly, "You may hope, sister. But do not expect... for such expectations seldom allow themselves become reality."

Hope watched his face, her expression rising and falling by the second. As he returned to listen to the men's conversation, she felt more crestfallen than before he had brought the glad tidings of the *Speedwell*'s fate. Her heart leapt toward the sky one moment before tumbling down to earth the next. She sat down abruptly on deck and rubbed her clammy hands together, finding it hard to wait for news concerning such a matter.

She gazed into the circle of men, who had met together in the fresh air on deck to discuss matters. "Oh, Father," she whispered, as she watched the back of his dark head. "If only I knew a way to convince you to return to Holland."

Stress mounted, and Hope found herself pacing one moment and sitting on the deck the next. Eventually she leaned against a barrel, her head falling back to look up at the sky. "I will hope, then," she muttered to herself and dreamed of Holland, with its quaint canals, its cheerful town homes, its delightful festivities, its bright gardens, Constance's smiling face...

"Hope," a voice murmured at her side.

She lifted her head and found herself opening her eyes. "Had I fallen asleep?" She blinked, finding John standing before her.

He smiled. "I think you did."

"Oh." She suddenly remembered her dreams and sat up wildly. "John! Are we staying or going?"

She studied his face, trying to find the answer written upon it. A brightness shone in his eyes, which caused her heart to rise.

He took a deep breath and hesitated before saying slowly, "We are going."

Her face froze, and she felt her heart crumble around the edges. "Going?" she breathed as disappointment threatened to send her into despair. "Going?" Her voice rose louder.

"Hope, calm—" John began, but Hope refused to listen. High hopes often end in failure, but her heart was not in a place to bear disappointment at the moment. She ran to the edge of the ship and pressed her palms against the splintered rail. "Going?" she muttered bitterly to herself as tears filled her eyes.

"Hope."

She turned and hid her face in the folds of John's cloak. "Why must we be going?" she whispered.

CHAPTER X
Disruptions

Hope gazed around the 'tween deck of the *Mayflower* as she cowered in a secluded corner. How crowded it was! And yet half of the crowd was full of those she knew not with queer rough ways and troubling language. Off to seek their fortune, John had told her, and were not a part of the homelike congregation Hope had known all her life.

Hope wished them to the bottom of the sea.

"Have dreadful troubles again, Hope, eh?" a voice asked from beside her.

She jumped a little and turned, finding herself face-to-face with Joshua. She scowled at him. "You have no sense of understanding."

"Ah, but I think he does," another voice from the opposite side contradicted.

She whirled and found John grinning at her impishly. "Come to plague me, did you?" she groaned.

"Actually," John replied, standing up, "we came to cheer you. We are headed up deck, for the weather is mild and the breeze refreshing and I daresay a romp would do you good. Come along, now, and do not resist," he said with mock sternness as he held out a hand.

Hope gave him a dirty look, but grasped his hand anyway and allowed him to pull her to her feet. The three made their way through the hold, dodging children and clearing the makeshift cabins made from scraps of wood and wool blankets. Hope scrambled up the ladder first and left John and Joshua to follow behind. Before either of them emerged, however, she ducked behind a barrel. She heard the boys climb up and stifled a chuckle as they stood dumbfounded for a moment.

"Hope!" A head popped around the corner, and a hand clutched her arm.

She squealed.

John burst into laughter. Hope glowered at him, while Joshua teased, "Ah, Hope, you can never succeed at All Hid."

"Oh, can't I?" she mocked, and pointed to him and John. "Perchance you two hide and *I* seek you. And I *will* find you immediately, no doubt," she called as the boys dashed off. She leaned her head on the barrel and closed her eyes, beginning to count softly. A few moments later she had reached fifty, and she began her search.

She made her way across the deck, peering around crates and behind barrels as she did so. Thirty minutes later she was seething as the boys were no where to be found. Plopping herself down by the rail for a rest, she tilted her head back and suddenly hooted. "I told you I would find you!" she shouted.

"You did not say it would take you half the day to do so, however," John replied as he and Joshua jumped off the rigging. They strode across deck and settled next to Hope, who found herself giggling in spite of herself.

However, after the general laughter wore off, she felt a twinge of fear in her chest and looked at her brother. "That was rather dangerous, was it not?"

"How do you mean, Hope? We were but a few feet off the deck—" John protested, but Hope interrupted. "I mean if one of the sailors caught you."

John glanced at her. "Why do you say that?"

"You know those swaggering men hate us, John," Hope replied scornfully, but she couldn't hide the anxiety in her voice.

The boys exchanged glances. "Oh, come now, Hope. If you stay out of their way, they will stay out of yours," John said lightly but seemed uneasy after Hope's remark. Uncannily, he tensed of a sudden, placing a hand gently on Hope's knee. She glanced around to see what troubled him and found herself gazing up at a sailor with a ruddy face and nasty grin. "Cain't wait to throw ye overboard when the sickness befalls ye to the death!"

"You shan't throw any one of us overboard," John replied coolly, while Hope remained frozen. "For the sea does not make us sick as it does some."

The sailor snarled and drew close to them. "Then I shall be pleased when we reach land and the Indians scalp ye," he whispered, fumes of rum rolling off his tongue.

Hope looked at him with wide eyes. "Indians?" she croaked.

The sailor narrowed his eyes. "*Indians*. Wild men who run about half-naked, killing all with the bloodiest death known to them. 'Tis an act they be fond of. They feel it makes man of themselves, I reckon." He paused and glanced sharply at Hope. "I reckon they be pleased a gal like ye would come and act as 'nuther bit o' bait for their hatchets."

Hope shuddered.

John suddenly sprang to his feet, clenching his fists. "'Man of themselves,' eh? I suppose you think you make 'man of yourself' by frightening innocent girls on matters better left untold."

The sailor swore, but John cut in the midst of his words, saying harshly, "I would appreciate you keep your filth to yourself and stay away from my sister, least of all, hence forward."

The man shot him a steely look, but John gazed back at him, seemingly undaunted. For a long agonizing moment, the two young men measured one another, their jaws set tight. Hope shivered as she peered at the sailor from behind John's tense form, and she felt Joshua shift closer to her.

At last the man moved on. He cursed under his breath and managed to shove John as he passed, an act that caused her brother to make a move toward him before stopping abruptly. He glanced back at Hope.

"That wretch!" Joshua muttered as the sailor drew out of earshot.

John relaxed his fingers and sat down next to them, taking a deep breath as the anger on his face melted away. Hope moved close to him, and he slipped an arm around her small shoulders.

"John," she whispered, fear beginning to claw at her throat, "are... are there truly Indians?"

"Hope," he began, rubbing a hand across his forehead.

"*Tell* me!" She clutched his arm.

He looked at her tense face a moment before saying reluctantly, "Yes, perchance. But, Hope, we are well prepared to meet them. 'Tis something we were aware of a long while ago, and we have thought the matter out thoroughly. Anyhow," he gave her a half-smile before saying forcefully, "they shan't kill you before they kill me, and *that* shall take some reckoning with." He flexed his muscles, causing Hope to burst into a fit of shaky laughter, warding off the fright that seemed to hang over their heads. However, the sailor's words had settled coldly in her chest, and she knew it shouldn't be free from her mind for a long while yet.

The breeze cooled Hope's cheeks as she sat on a barrel, gasping for breath after a rowdy game of Lummelen with the other children. The day was mild and pleasant. Hope took a deep breath of salty air. Suddenly she shrieked as her head was jerked back, and she whipped around, finding—with no surprise—the mischievously grinning face of Francis Billington. "Foolish boy!" she snapped, spotting her mob cap dangling from his fingertips. "Return my coif at once!"

He wiggled his eyebrows, making a face at her before darting off. "Come fetch it!" he called tauntingly, and Hope stamped her foot. She glanced around for John, but he was nowhere in sight. Neither was Joshua, and remembering that Mother wasn't in view to scold her, she ran after Francis.

Unfortunately, the vexing lad had the advantage, for his breeches allowed him to leap over crates and overturned barrels, while Hope's petticoats held her back. For a long while the game kept on, until at last Francis slowed. Hope

Cry of Hope

threw herself toward her possession just as Francis stepped aside, and she screeched as a barrel loomed in front of her. She leapt, nearly clearing the rim when her petticoat snagged, and she tumbled quite ceremoniously to the ground, scraping her knees on the rough wood and plummeting prostrate across deck.

"Hope Ellison!"

It was a familiar gasp, and Hope groaned inwardly. She stubbornly chose to lie where she was and managed to fight back tears due to her smarting hands and knees.

A moment later she was pulled to her feet, and Mother stared stonily down at her. Hope returned the favor.

A long silence fell until Mother asked, without a scar of gentleness piercing her provoked tone, "Where is your coif?"

Hope refused to answer, anger boiling in her veins. Instead, she pointed toward Francis Billington, who stood among the group of children watching the scene. Mother stepped toward the lad and held out her hand. Francis meekly placed Hope's mob cap in it. Hope raised her chin and looked away.

"I think it is high time you retire for the evening," Mother said tersely, placing her hands on Hope's shoulders and pushing her toward the ladder. Hope obeyed without a word.

A tiny squeal met her as she stepped into the 'tween deck, and she looked inquiringly into Mother's face.

"Goodwife Hopkins just gave birth," she whispered hurriedly.

Hope clapped a hand over her mouth. "Might I see the baby, Mother?" she pleaded, reverting suddenly to a meek expression. "Merely a glimpse?"

"Retire to your hammock," Mother replied sternly, and Hope fought back angry tears as she scuttled to her bed and collapsed into it. She pulled her coverlet over her face to hide herself and lay awake for several hours. Then, as the late afternoon finally slipped into late evening, she fell asleep, with the tantalizing smells of cheese and bread tickling her nose.

"What shall his name be?"

Hope stood by Goodwife Hopkins' side the next morning, gazing down into the face of the beautiful newborn. He lay swaddled in his mother's arms, uncannily quiet and quite visibly frightened by all of the attention he was receiving. Hope gingerly reached out with one finger, stroking his tiny hand. He did not grasp it, but lay staring at her with large blue eyes. She gave him an encouraging smile.

"We are unsure as of yet," Goodman Hopkins responded to the question asked by Mother, who stood hovering over the child.

John stepped behind Hope and peered down at the baby.

"Is he not precious?" she whispered shyly to him.

"That he is," he smiled, placing a hand on her shoulder. "I remember when you were that tiny, Hope. You frightened everyone with your incessant squeals."

Hope was indignant but couldn't hide her grin. "More than likely I did so because you encouraged it," she returned.

"Now do I appear so foolish as that?" John shot back, his brown eyes twinkling.

Hope shoved his arm.

They gazed down at the little child a moment longer. Hope then noticed the lull in the conversation between Goodwife Hopkins and Mother and quickly spoke. "Might I hold him?"

Goodwife Hopkins looked at her and smiled. "Indeed, dear. You must be very careful with this little bundle." She began to hand him to Hope.

"No, Hope."

She looked up, her mouth dropping. Goodwife Hopkins looked questioningly at Mother.

"I do not believe you are capable, dear."

Cheeks blazing, Hope stared at Mother. She searched her face, wondering if she was still under punishment for her act upon deck yesterday. She wasn't. Mother no longer looked stony nor stern. Instead, a forlorn look shone in her eyes, and she said softly, "You have not shown yourself competent in womanly deeds, child."

Hope felt hot tears of shame rise in her eyes, and she ran away. She ran to the corner of the 'tween deck and flung herself across her hammock, burying her face in her arms. Her lips trembled as she tried to hold back the tears. She glanced back where Goodwife Hopkins lay. She watched as the lady handed the baby to her daughter Constanta, a sturdy young girl Hope's age. Tears ran down her cheeks unchecked.

Suddenly a warm hand settled on her back, and she turned. John sat down on a crude wooden stool, drawing her toward him. She buried her face in his shoulder, and he let her cry. For quite a while she wept bitter tears, until finally he said softly, "Mother meant no harm, little sister. She is afraid to allow you to handle such a gentle creature. To her, you are still a child, not yet ready to become a woman. And perhaps so." He was quiet a moment, and Hope clutched his neck tightly. "I think, however," he said, setting her back and resting his hands on her shoulders. "I think you are more capable than even you could surmise. You will grow into an accomplished young woman yet. Of that I am sure."

Hope gazed at him a moment before smiling in spite of herself. John grinned and brushed the tears off her cheeks, then tousled her hair. They both gazed back toward the little baby. Mother was now holding him, caressing his cheeks with a look of pure delight on her face. Suddenly Goodman Hopkins cleared his throat after conversing with one of the men. "His name," he announced distinctly, "shall be Oceanus."

"Oceanus," Hope whispered. She looked at John and grinned. "How fitting."

CHAPTER XI

The Sea's Roar

"I declare, the monotony is apt to drive *someone* bizarre," Hope said bitterly a few weeks later, as the novelty of sailing on the *Mayflower* had quickly worn off, and she was left with a hopeless amount of time on her hands and nothing to do with it.

"Stranger things have happened," John laughed.

"I rather hope it *does* happen," Joshua said with a twinkle in his eye, "for it would then drive away our monotony in the amusement of watching the unfortunate fellow."

"Shan't, though," Patience sniffed, "for such things are not at all likely."

Hope glared at her.

Suddenly something heavy hit her ankle, and the next moment a sailor came crashing down on deck before her. Hope's mouth dropped open in shock, and the silence behind her evinced that her brother and Joshua were just as surprised as she. A head of flyaway red hair slipped down the ladder in fright a little ahead of them, and Patience's retreating figure disappeared from sight. Scoffs arose in Hope's throat from such fear, but the next moment she found herself trembling in terror as she knew what consequences the man would befall on her after causing him to stumble in such a way.

Suddenly she realized he had moved not an inch since his fall. With a start, she snapped her legs back from their reclining position and glanced at her brother with large eyes, wondering what was wrong with the fellow. John glanced at Joshua for a moment, then leapt forward and shook the sailor's shoulder. "Are you harmed, sir?" he asked, but a little shake to his voice squeezed Hope's stomach with fear.

"D-did *I* harm him?" she whispered, hugging her knees to her chest and feeling suddenly cold.

"No!" John snapped and nudged the man again.

Hot tears stung her eyes. "I *did* harm him," she whispered, hiding her face in her petticoat.

"Now, now," Joshua said gently behind her, "you haven't harmed the fellow, Hope, so pull yourself together." He stepped forward and knelt next to the man while Hope tried to choke down the wails that arose in her throat. Feeling his forehead for a moment, Joshua looked up. "He is ill, John," he told his friend.

"Sicker than a wet dog," John replied disdainfully. "No less than he deserves, however."

Hope looked up slowly as he uttered the words and whispered, "Is *he* the one whom threatened us?"

John nodded. "Best to get him to his cabin, I suppose," he said, glancing at Joshua, who followed his movements. Together, the two boys began to carry the sailor to the cabin. John called over his shoulder, "Notify the ship's surgeon, Hope. He needs assistance."

Hope nodded numbly and ran off, knowing not where the man might be; but her legs decided that for her. She found herself bursting into the ship master's cabin a moment later, crying out somewhat incoherently, "A sailor has fallen ill! My brother is taking him to the cabin! Please, he needs the ship's surgeon!"

Christopher Jones looked up at her sharply, from where he had been studying a map with two other men, and barked, "This cabin is strictly off your limits, child!"

"But, sir, my brother—" she protested wildly, rather out of her sane mind, but he cut her off by turning to one of the men. "See what the wretch is speaking of and take the matters into your own hands."

"Aye, sir." The man began to lead Hope out of the room, but she fought him, crying out, "I *need* the ship's surgeon! My brother sent me!"

"Hush, child!" the man replied sharply, as he closed the heavy door behind him. "I *am* the ship's surgeon."

Hope's eyes widened, but she was silent from then onward and submissively followed the man down the ladder into the cabin which the sailors occupied.

The boys had just laid the sorry fellow on a bunk. Hope gasped when she saw the man's rugged face, so red with heat and beaded with perspiration that she felt her stomach turn over sourly. He lay motionless, until he suddenly jerked his fists out wildly, knocking one into the wall of the cabin while the other slammed a solid blow into Joshua's chin. Hope screamed.

"Get the child *out*, son!" the ship's surgeon demanded. John turned to obey. "No, not you!" The surgeon threw up his arms. "You." He pointed to Joshua, who stood stunned from the force of the blow.

Joshua nodded silently and led Hope up the ladder, who trembled so much she could hardly clutch the rungs. "Oh, Joshua!" she cried, upon reaching the deck. He glanced down at her with a half-smile, silently rubbing his bruised jaw. "I suppose my wish came true in some respects. That fellow seems to have gone rather bizarre," he told her wryly.

Hope glanced at him sharply, a smile suddenly tickling her lips. He grinned back and settled down, leaning against a barrel. "Shall we wait until your brother comes out? I believe the ship's surgeon has given him the duty of holding the sailor down."

She nodded and sat next to him, leaning her chin on her knees. They sat in silence for some time, listening to the sloshing water against the ship and the wild snapping of the sails overhead. Hope tilted her head back, gazing up at the mild blue sky, wider and clearer than the ocean that surrounded them on all sides.

It was quite a long while before John came up, but when he did, his sober attitude was rather alarming.

"Is it worse than expected?" Joshua asked quietly.

"Rather," John replied grimly. He glanced at Hope, before saying slowly, "Do you recall how he taunted us, saying that he was eager to throw us overboard before the journey's end?"

They nodded.

"It appears it has turned against him. Of all the irony, that young sailor is the first to be buried beneath the cold ocean waters."

Like a shot through the night, Hope was suddenly jolted out of her sleep. "John?" she asked cautiously, sitting up and gazing around the room. Nothing met her eyes but pitch black air that threatened to smother her. Movement could be heard around the room, and hushed urgent voices reached her ears. She grew thoroughly alarmed and began to step out of her hammock when suddenly she was thrown against the wall.

"John!" she shrieked as a noise like thunder drowned out her words and left her clinging to a barrel in terror. She leaned her forehead against her arms and began shaking. "John, where are you? Mother? Father! Father, do you hear me?"

In a moment a pair of arms wrapped around her shaking form, and a familiar voice said in her ear, "I am here, Hope."

She hid her face in John's shoulder and clung to him. Suddenly the ship gave a terrible lurch, sending them both sprawling on the floor.

"John! Hope!" It was Father shouting for them. Water began trickling in from the tight cracks in the low ceiling overhead as Hope cried out, "I am here, Father!" She trembled, inching her way across the floor on her knees. By now the storm was raging, and the ship rocked so violently Hope felt her stomach turning sour. A crash sounded just ahead, and she screamed as an overturned trunk slid toward her.

Suddenly strong arms grasped her by the waist. "Hope!" It was Father. "Stay with John, do you understand me?" he shouted. "Stay with John!" He had her held tightly against his shoulder, and she sobbed, nodding her head. John took her in his arms then, and Father helped them into the corner. John braced himself against the wall and took Hope upon his lap. He wrapped his arms tightly around her as a crack of thunder split their eardrums.

"Where is Father going?" Hope sobbed into John's ear, trembling.

"To help Mother."

Another growl of thunder threatened them from overhead, and Hope buried her face in her brother's shoulder. They clung to one another. Stench rose in the air from the seasickness of fellow voyagers, and with another violent lurch, Hope found herself in the clutches of the awful malady herself. When she was finished, her head felt queer, and she found herself growing dizzy. "John!" she cried out suddenly, grasping his neck. "John, we shall go under!"

"We will be alright, Hope," he said, gasping as a spray of salty seawater poured down upon their heads.

Hope sputtered. "You do not know so!"

"Hope," he said into her ear, as the ship creaked warningly, "I promised."

And with those final words, Hope was sucked up by a queer force and dragged numbly into a whirling, swirling darkness.

CHAPTER XII

Oppression

"Praise God we are sound," John said quietly the next morning. The siblings were leaning on the rail, peering out over the waters. The day was cloudy but calm, and Hope took gulping breaths of the fresh air after the reek of the 'tween deck.

The rough, choppy waters of the ocean bounced the ship about, but Mother had consented to their request to go upon deck, provided that John watch carefully for any signs of a storm, and that they come down immediately if there were.

Hope sighed dejectedly, letting her arms dangle limp over the rail. "How much longer until we reach the New World?" she asked for the first time since their leaving.

John rubbed his face with his hands, shaking his head. "I do not know. I should speculate two or three more weeks, but as I said a long while ago, sea life is always full of uncertainty."

"I do not like it," Hope said crossly, staring at the cruel horizon shrouded with gloomy clouds. She shivered as a cold wind whipped her hair out of its knot, sending tangles into her face. She pushed them back impatiently and looked at John.

He was staring up at the sky, concern etched on his face. "I do not like the looks of it," he murmured, slowly taking Hope's wrist. "I think perhaps—" A sudden flash blinded their eyes, and a crack of thunder swallowed his words.

Hope screamed. The ship began to rock violently, and John gripped her shoulders, saying hurriedly, "Come, Hope, run!"

The ladder to the 'tween deck lay but a few yards away, and the siblings darted toward it. However, the storm was picking up, and halfway across deck the ship lurched incredibly, sent them sprawling toward the mast. John scrambled to his feet, grabbing Hope's arms and pulling her up.

Suddenly a howl echoed across deck. Hope caught John's arm as he whipped around. A blurred glimpse of a voyager tumbling over the side of the ship ignited a scream out of Hope. John pushed her to the ground, calling out, "Grasp the rigging, and do not let go!"

"No!" she cried. He stumbled away from her, toward the side of the ship. "John, you shall fall overboard!" she screamed and took a few steps after him. Just then a wave crashed upon deck, and Hope lost view of John as salty foam dashed her face. She shrieked as she began to slip backward. Blindly reaching out in front of her, she managed to grasp the thick rope of the rigging. Tears streaked her face as she desperately searched for John.

"Hope!"

Father appeared at her side, wrapping his arms around

her.

"Father!" she gasped, clinging to him. "Father, someone fell overboard, and John—"

He said not another word but sprang to the ladder, pushing her down.

"Father, save John!" she screamed after him, delirium setting in as another wave crashed over the side of the ship, and Father was lost from view.

Hands grabbed her around the waist, and she wept bitterly as Joshua helped her down the ladder. Mother met her at the bottom rung and swathed her in a blanket.

"Mother, John and Father are out there!" Hope wailed, shaking from head to foot.

Mother said not another word but clenched her shoulders tightly.

For an agonizing while, the storm howled overhead with no return of the men, and Hope's face paled as thought after horrible thought plummeted into her head. John could not have disappeared beneath the ocean waters. He could not. Father... Hope sat abruptly on the floor, breathing heavily as memories flooded over her and fears rose within her. She buried her face in the blanket.

A hand touched her shoulder, and she looked up.

Patience Danford stared down at her. Her dark eyes were wide in her slight face, and she sat down heavily on a wooden barrel, rocking herself back and forth. "They will die," Hope caught the words Patience mumbled to herself. "They will die again."

Hope felt her fear reach a breaking point, and she leapt to her feet, rage boiling through her veins. "Do not say such foolish things, you wretch!" she wailed, tears streaking her face. "Now is not the time for one of your breakdowns! Cease at once!" She collapsed again to the floor, weeping uncontrollably.

Mother sat down next to her, grabbing her daughter's head with trembling hands and pulling it to her chest. "I ought to punish you," she whispered fiercely in Hope's ear, her reproof slipping into a sob. "I ought to punish you." And her grip on Hope's arms grew tighter and tighter.

Suddenly the hatch flew open. Water poured in from above. Hope scrambled dizzily to her feet. "John! Father!" she cried. "John, please!" Her voice broke as tears blurred her vision.

The next moment a voice was whispering in her ear, "'Tis alright, little sister. I am here." She threw herself in his arms, gripping his neck as she buried her face in his shoulder. Her eyes were blurred for a long moment, but when she looked up, she saw Mother clinging to Father. It was then that she spotted the drenched man from their congregation wrapped in a blanket a few feet away.

"Did you save him?" she faltered.

"John Howland?" He set her down and looked at the man. "No. God did."

"Another storm is brewing," John said grimly several days later.

Hope shuddered and could have burst into tears just then if Joshua hadn't said comically, "I suppose that means we go another day without eating?"

Queerly enough, his words made her smile in spite

of the circumstances, and John replied with a short laugh, "I generally worry not about eating during a storm."

Joshua shrugged. "I suppose, but it really causes one to worry about eating beforehand." He pointed to the hardtack in his hand with a frown.

Hope rubbed her stomach, saying, "I propose we give up on eating until we reach the New World."

Joshua's lips curved in a wry smile. He nodded wordlessly, tossing the victual back in the barrel and settling down against the side of the ship, as if submissively waiting for the storm to come.

Father approached them a moment later. "Stay together," he instructed. "Do not separate. Do you hear me, John? Do not let your sister out of your sight for an instant."

"Yes, sir."

Father dwindled into the shadows, just as the hatch was securely shut. The dreary light of the 'tween deck was extinguished with the thump of its closure.

Hope huddled next to John, and he slipped an arm firmly around her shoulders. A low rumble of thunder was heard overhead. Hope's stomach squeezed, and she closed her eyes fearfully.

The 'tween deck fell eerily silent, as all waited for the storm to send the ship into the rolling ocean waters. "John," Hope whispered, panic beginning to rise in her throat, "suppose we do not emerge from the storm?"

"We will be alright, Hope."

"How do you *know?*"

He brushed back a strand of her dark hair. "Faith assures such things."

She cuddled closer to him, grasping his arm with a

fierce clutch. A crack of thunder sounded overhead, and the ship gave a sharp lurch as a wave rose under it. Hope hid her face in his shoulder, her grip on his arm growing all the harsher. "'Twill be alright, Hope," he whispered in her ear, but his voice was drowned out by another groan from the sky above, and the vessel began to jerk as the steep waves tossed it severely about.

"What a fool," Hope heard Joshua moan from the other side of John. "What a fool I was to eat beforehand." And had her stomach not begun feeling horridly sour as well, she would have cracked a smile.

It was then that the storm suddenly exploded. Lightening pricked the waters, igniting an intense thunder that burst forth from overhead. Hope screamed as it seared through her eardrums and caused the surfaces around her to shudder from the immense force. John's arm tightened around Hope, and she clung desperately to his frame as the ship was wrenched about in the churning waters.

Sporadic jerks sent Hope's body flying in air and then sailing back down to the floor with a slam that stole her breath from her. John tried his best to keep her steady, but just then the heavens opened up with desperate torrents. Dashes of salty water were suddenly flung into Hope's face, and she choked as it burned her nostrils and throat. It was heaved up a moment later, only to be returned again with a spray of the sickening water. Gasping and soaking, Hope tried shielding herself from the stormy elements by burying her face in John's shoulder, and eventually he pulled her onto his lap, wrapping his arms around her in protection. Hope's eyes stung with salt and tears, and a familiar numbing sensation began to overcome her as the storm wore on.

Cry of *Hope*

Suddenly a terrific splintering could be heard above. An earsplitting crack sent a gush of water flooding the 'tween deck. Hope cried out in terror. The next moment another lurch sent the ship spinning in the rising waves, and Hope's head flew up, slamming against the ship's side. She plummeted into a dizzying darkness.

Hope stirred. Her head throbbed terribly, and she wondered why she felt so uncomfortably damp and cold.

"Hope?"

It was a familiar voice, and her eyelids flickered. She blinked, seeing John's concerned brown eyes peering down at her. "Mother, she has awakened."

A quick step was heard, and Mother's worried face appeared. "Oh, Hope!" she gasped, her hand touching Hope's forehead.

Hope winced.

"Is she very harmed?"

John passed a hand over his eyes, his shoulders drooping. "I do not know."

"John, fetch the ship's surgeon, please," Mother pleaded, setting herself on a crude stool by Hope's hammock.

John stood to go, but suddenly a large hand clamped on his shoulder. He turned, facing his father.

"I bid you to watch out for her," Father said between clenched teeth, his voice eerily hushed.

John shook his head, and Hope was astonished to see tears trembling in his dark eyes. "I tried, Father," he hissed, looking him in the eye. "I tried. You know a man can be at fault unintentionally. You know that full well."

Father glowered at him, gripping his shoulders. John stared back, his eyes blazing. Then Father's lips trembled, and he shoved John back, stomping into the shadows.

John caught hold of a support. He hid his face a moment, then turned back to Hope and Mother. "I will fetch the ship's surgeon," he muttered, turning quickly and disappearing up the ladder.

Hope looked at Mother. "I think my head is not so very harmed," she whispered. She rolled over and pulled the coverlet up to her chin, her face pinched with pain.

The ship's surgeon arrived shortly. He gently examined Hope's head. Finally he turned to Mother and murmured, "A nasty bruise, that is. Do not allow her out of her bed for a full week and try to bathe it with heated saltwater. I shall be back in a few days." He peered around the crowded, disconsolate 'tween deck. "Dirty place, this is. 'Tis a wonder we did not disappear beneath the ocean last evening. 'Tis a wonder."

"'Tis an act of God," Mother replied firmly.

The ship's surgeon shrugged. "Remember my instructions," he said, then turned and tramped toward the ladder.

John appeared a moment later. "Let me relieve you, Mother."

Mother sighed, her pale face worried. "As you wish, son." She rose and went away, presumably to heat saltwater on the metal brazier.

John looked down at Hope. "How are you faring?" he asked softly.

Hope shrugged, biting her lip. "How did we survive

the storm?"

John sighed. "'Twasn't easy." He then told her softly of the events that took place after Hope had knocked her head against the ship's side: how he had nearly panicked when Hope would not respond to his touch, how the terrifying noise had indicated the main beam's breakage, how they began to wonder if the storm wouldn't shatter the entire ship before the beam was fixed, and how the iron screw was used to repair the dangerous damage.

"The men did the job splendidly, despite the wild winds," John finished. "I could not leave you so limp and pale, and the ship rocked much too violently for me to search for Mother or Father. I had begun to think we would truly go under."

Hope gazed up at the splintered ceiling.

Suddenly a boyish voice spoke sprightly nearby. "Ah, Hope has been returned to us!"

John glanced at his friend. "That she has, thank God." He looked down at Hope. She smiled as he whispered again, "Thank God."

CHAPTER XIII
A Glimpse of Hope

"Must I eat it?" Hope whimpered a few weeks later.

Though she had had many awful days throughout the voyage, she felt this to be the most unruly. She had awakened before dawn shivering. Her head ached from cold so terribly that she could not fall back asleep, and just before the sun broke over the horizon, another cloud of storms overtook them. For several hours the storm raged on, and though John held her safely through it, his strong arms didn't keep her from becoming drenched and unnerved.

Now, having been informed that the cheese was entirely unfit to eat, she could not bear to curb her stomach pangs with hardtack, for she had to suck on the nasty victual for a long while before it was soft enough to chew.

"*Must* I eat it?" she asked groggily again.

John glanced at her. "If you do not, you will acquire nothing else."

Hope sat trembling for a moment, her mind swimming. Suddenly she flung the hardtack to the floor with a clatter and burst into frantic tears. Paying no mind to the shocked faces that settled over her, she ran out of the 'tween deck, collapsing on deck. "'Tis *hateful!*" she sobbed, burying her face in her arms. "'Tis *hateful!*"

"Hope?"

She made no response, but the tears began to come more rapidly with bitterness and exhaustion. "I want it to be *over!*" she gasped.

"So do I."

"No, no, not over in the New World! I want it to be over! I want to feel safe! I want to feel comfort! I want to be *home!*" she cried. She tried to stop the flow of tears, but her breath came in ragged gasps; she found it wouldn't be so. "Oh, John!" she gasped and flung her head onto his shoulder, wailing miserably.

He made no response but stroked her hair soothingly.

"P-please!" she cried, choking on hot tears. "Please take me home!"

"We will be home soon."

"No! Not the New World! The New World will *never* be home!" Hope sobbed, her heart painfully beating against her chest.

"Have you lost hope, little sister?" he asked softly, after a short pause.

The tears streamed down her face, and she gave a slight nod. "I-I," she stuttered, "I *cannot* go on!"

He was silent. "Do you remember what I told you, Hope?" he asked at last.

She made no response, but gave another gasp.

"Hope," he turned, taking her face in his hands and looking her in the eye. "As long as we have faith, hope can never die."

She gazed at him. He gave a slight smile, brushing aside the tears that stung her cheeks with bitter droplets. His brown eyes grew sad, and he swallowed. "As long as we have faith, Hope," he repeated, "hope can *never* die. Do you understand?"

She said nothing, but her weeping began to cease. She rested her head on his shoulder, and the tears that rolled down her cheeks grew slower and gentler. Suddenly she felt her body grow limp with exhaustion. She felt the rough shirtsleeve rub across her cheek as John stood, and she allowed him to carry her below deck where he gently placed her in a hammock. Then he turned and left her to fall asleep as the ship rocked the makeshift bed back and forth until it lulled her into a deep slumber.

***

The cold air suddenly settled down on them. Hope felt it first when she awoke one morning, finding herself shivering. "What—" she began to say, when she noticed her breath coming in white clouds from her mouth, shriveling away an instant later. Her eyes widened, and she took in a deep breath, feeling the marked change in the air around her. It was cold and colourless and so crisp that it stung her lungs with a sharp sting.

She shivered again. She heard John coughing nearby and turned to him, exclaiming, "'Tis *cold!*"

He laughed, waking the cheery warmth that sometimes does more good. "Is it now?" he grinned, stepping toward her and rubbing his hands briskly over his arms. "'Tis indeed, I must say, but all we need is a quick run on the deck to bring the chill out of your bones. Come with me?"

"But, John, the storms."

"'Tis a clear morning at the moment, and I shall keep my eyes attuned to any change the weather may bring. Come along, now."

"The sailors—"

"Keep away from the wretches, and they shall keep away from you. Come *along*, Hope."

So Hope gave a reluctant sigh and followed him toward the ladder.

As she stepped out on deck, she was nearly knocked backward from the blast of glacial air that cut through her skin, seeping into the very marrows of her bones until they ached uncontrollably. She tried to gasp, but her lungs seemed to have frozen. She slapped her chest frantically to beat them back into motion.

"Just breathe," a voice said close by. She turned, following John's pattern of taking one deep breath and letting it out slowly, one deep breath and letting it out slowly, relaxing the tensed lungs into working order.

"See? 'Tis not so hard," John grinned, leaning his arm on a barrel. "But..." he glanced at her impishly, "*'tis* hard to catch your brother in a race."

He grinned and leapt off, as Hope screeched and followed suit, racing as fast as her shorter legs could to catch up with his long strides. "'Tisn't *fair!*" she cried, though she rather sang it out gaily in the frigid air, feeling as if her cheerful spirit taunted the cold in a very satisfactory way.

"Perchance," John replied, slowing, and allowed Hope to nearly catch up to him. "Or perchance not." He threw her mischievous gleam and took off on full speed again, causing

Hope to stop for a moment, stamping her foot in frustration. However, an instant later she was following him again with a grin tickling her lips. She never could run a race without smiling in spite of her poor skills.

At long last she caught up with John, who must have become winded, for he stopped abruptly at the rail. She gasped, wiping her nose, and said, "Supposed I would not catch you, eh?" She grinned.

He turned his head slightly toward her but did not remove his gaze from the horizon. "Y-yes," he said absently, "I suppose so."

Hope looked at him curiously. He was squinting hard. Suddenly he snapped his fingers, saying sharply, "Fetch me a spyglass."

"W-what?" Hope asked, startled.

"A spyglass, I need one." He glanced around frantically, finally spotting one lying carelessly by the rigging. In a bound he was on it, and he grasped it, peering up at the ropes. He hesitated only a moment before astonishing Hope as he secured the spyglass around his waist and climbed ably up.

"John Ellison!" she croaked, her mouth dropping as she watched his figure grow smaller and smaller as he scrambled high into the air. Her eyes darted around anxiously, but no sailors seemed to be in sight, though she knew very well they should be.

She shaded her eyes from the hazy winter sun and squinted as she saw her brother climb into the crow's nest, holding the glass capably to his eye. "What is he *doing?*" she whispered to herself.

Suddenly she saw him drop the spyglass onto the slim deck beneath his feet and wring his hands together as if agitated. The next his arm clumsily grabbed the spyglass again before he bellowed, "Land ho!"

Hope's mouth dropped. *Land ho?* She shook her head. "No, no," she whispered, "it can't be true, it—" She glanced up to see John waving his arms and shouting out the tidings once again. The next moment her vision blurred, and she realized tears were streaming down her face. Her legs grew shaky and collapsed from under her. She leaned her head on her knees, rocking back and forth as tears flowed from her heart. "Land!" she whispered incoherently. "Land! here! Land! land!"

An instant later, the deck was swarmed with commotion, as the voyagers came up, cheering, crying, and giving thanks to God fervently. But Hope sat on deck in the midst of them, doing nothing but burying her face in her skirt, shaking. An arm slipped around her shoulders a moment later and pulled her to her feet. She scrubbed a few tears from her stained eyes and found John smiling triumphantly down upon her. "Land, Hope," he said shakily, and she gave a hysterical little laugh, leaping to fling her arms around his neck. "Land!"

"You mean we are not settling *there?*" Hope implored, waving her arm toward the coast ahead of them, now much clearer after sailing steadily toward it for the past few hours.

"No, we think we may attempt to sail down to the Hudson River and settle along there, as the weather appears clear for sailing to-day," John replied, leaning his arms merrily on the railing, unfazed by the glacial wind that threatened to chap their faces frozen.

"Why so?" Hope asked, rubbing her hands together and noticing that they were turning a faint purplish colour from the cold, dry air.

"We had originally intended on settling further south, but the storms blew us off course. Father and the men have conversed, and they have agreed 'twould be best to settle along the river than directly on the coast here at Cape Cod," John explained, gesturing to the land that seemed so inviting just ahead. "So we shall sail further south until we reach it."

"You mean," Hope replied slowly, her face falling, "I shan't so much as touch the solid ground until we have sailed still further?"

John tossed her a grin. "Correct, sister. You *do* think so logically."

Hope attempted to glare at him in vexation, but she couldn't hold back a laugh. "How long *must* it be until we reach the Hudson River?" she asked momentarily.

"In this fair weather, I would presume only a day or two. However, storms have proved themselves such fickle things that one can never be too sure."

Hope's lips curved. "I wish storms would never plague us again," she said, subconsciously rubbing her stomach. "One would think that after constantly beating upon us for—how many weeks? Five?—they would kindly relent just a little."

John shrugged as a sharp breeze suddenly whipped his cloak about. He leaned against the railing, crossing his arms. "And what do you think of that beautiful greenery ahead, Hope?" His eyes shone as he gazed out toward the land, a wide expanse of vast wilderness.

Hope slowly nodded, taking in the view as a spray of

salty sea water smarted her eyes. "'Tis the New World, that is for certain."

John laughed. A rumble of thunder growled in the distance, causing him to sober of a sudden. His eyes darted to the sky; a groan escaped his lips. "I think..." He paused a moment, before saying resolutely, "Another storm is coming."

Hope's mouth dropped. Her eyes swept the sky, and she noticed for the first time the rapidly changing weather. Angry clouds churned bitterly, fast approaching them from the southeast.

"Why must it?" she moaned, but John suddenly grasped her hand and pulled her across the deck toward the 'tween deck. Another thunderclap came from overhead. The pale sun disappeared as a dark gloom settled over the ocean.

Hope scrambled to keep up with her brother's long strides. A bright flash lit up the dreariness, and though Hope braced herself, the crack of thunder that followed sounded more menacing than she had expected. She found her feet pounding all the faster. *A storm!* she thought with a mixture of anger and fear and exhaustion. *Oh, fool of a storm!*

The storm, however, did not appear to be foolish in any sense of the word. As soon as John and Hope had retreated to the safety of shelter, it seemed to collapse upon them. Hope was scrambling down the ladder when the ship gave a terrible lurch that sent her sprawling to the floor. John, who had scarcely shut the hatch, more or less leapt down after her and pulled her next to him as he held tight to the ladder.

"Oh!" moaned Hope, as the rain began to creep upon the deck above them. "Why must it storm now?"

"So I am asking," John muttered. "We are far too near the rocky shore for me to feel any bit comfortable."

Hope's eyes widened, and her mouth dropped. Before she had time to blurt out any of the fears that crept into her throat, a smash of thunder scathed her unspoken words, and water poured down upon their heads as the hatch flew open.

"John!" Her shriek pierced through the storm's increasing din.

Her brother dropped hold of her and scrambled to close it, leaving Hope shivering in terror as she grasped one of the ladder rungs. Suddenly another figure lunged at him out of the shadows. Father clapped his hand on John's shoulder and flung him back to the floor. "Get back, son!" he roared, as a wave crashed into the 'tween deck, hurling icy saltwater into Hope's face. She choked and fell backward, knocking into a barrel. John shrank back with her, and they both strained their eyes searching for the faint outline of Father attempting to close the hatch.

Hope spotted him just as another figure came into view. "We—turning back—rocky cli—!" The screaming waters washed out many of the words, but Hope closed her eyes in trembling as she understood clearly what the sailor had meant. Tears rolled down her cheeks as a spray of water spat in her face. She leaned her forehead against John's arm, feeling her relief to be near solid ground shriveling away.

Father soon had the hatch securely closed, and he stepped down as the ship again careened. He stumbled into the shadows, where Hope caught sight of Mother's terrified face, a tear glinting on her cheek in the light of the brazier. Hope was watching him wrap his arms around her when the flame inside the metal warmer was extinguished. The 'tween deck slipped into utter blackness. She grabbed John's arm then, and he squeezed her shoulder reassuringly. They could do nothing but wait out the storm.

Outside the tight walls of the ship, the angry sea pounded against the rocky surf, churning and slashing at the sharp rocks with a stinging spray. The *Mayflower* pitched about, unintentionally caught in the fierce battle between land and water. Screeching waves burst upon rocky bights, exploding in a cloud of saltwater. Shots of roaring sea were flung onto the edge of the bluffs, from which they were hurled back down again, writhing in utter fury. Stones and pebbles were tossed about in the turmoil, sporadically bouncing against cliffs or penetrating the soft wood of the ship caught amidst it all. The solid rocks spat back at the enraged ocean, standing like a barricade against the land which they protected. Determined and strong, they refused to cede it to the hands of the mighty ocean, and they jeered and taunted the offender with almost lifelike snarls.

The unfortunate predicament the *Mayflower* became entangled in grew frighteningly precarious as the heedless ocean and defensive land closed in on them from both sides, wedging together until merely a breath of wind or an inch of rolling wave would send them shattering onto a sharp rock. Breathlessly Hope clung to John in the 'tween deck. All seemed to be waiting for the inevitable, even the sailors who worked feverishly upon deck.

Then, wonder of wonders, the *Mayflower* rolled back. The sea still churned around them, but the roar of breakers against boulders eased from hearing range, and the *Mayflower*'s fiercest struggle was over. Hope breathed a sigh of relief and dropped her head upon John's shoulder. "Thank God the worst is over," he sighed fervently, brushing his damp forehead where saltwater trickled down. "Thank God."

CHAPTER XIV
Til Paths Be Wrought

Hope strained her eyes toward land. Only a few more waves would wash the shallop onto the shore of Cape Cod. She shivered in excitement, her chapped cheeks rosy in the wind. She glanced at John. He grinned at her, gripping his musket. The men had explored the shore for a short distance two days before, but with the women and children now landing for the washing, they felt the need for several men to accompany them with sufficient weaponry.

At the moment, Hope was too excited to think long about dangers.

With a scrape, the shallop had landed on the firm beach. John leapt out of the boat, followed by the other men, and they dragged her ashore. Hope closed her eyes. They were on solid ground.

She took a deep breath, as if tasting life for the first time since boarding the *Mayflower*. Her feet tingled, and she suddenly sprang from her seat and over the side onto the beach, ignoring Mother's reproofs for acting in a most horridly boyish manner.

Suddenly she found herself sprawled on the sand, and she gazed about in a daze, wondering how she had stumbled. She heard a hearty laugh from above and glanced up. John's eyes twinkled down at her. "How—" she began, but he interrupted her with the cheerful reminder, "Sea legs have trouble adjusting to land."

Hope scowled and attempted to stand but found herself spinning and spinning, and she promptly fell on her knees again. She groaned. "I suppose a romp is out of the question."

John grinned. "Oh, come now," he replied, reaching out his hand. "All you need is practice, and you will be fitter on land than sea once again."

Hope couldn't suppress a smile, and she grasped his hand and stood. "Now then," he said, letting go. Suddenly he seemed to think better of it, as Hope began to sway, and readily grabbed her arm again. "Take a step," he ordered, and Hope did so, though she clung to his arm. "Do so again," he commanded as she stopped, looking dizzy. He pulled her forward another step. "There," he said. "Now run."

"What?"

"Run."

And Hope was suddenly dragged into the queerest, most dizzying romp she had ever taken part in. She felt her eyes spinning, for the land dipped dreadfully, and she would have toppled down like a little child had John not kept firm hold of her arm. At length, however, John's method proved best, and she began to run on her own. Her eyes focused, and her heart rose higher and higher in her throat as she ran as fast and as hard as her legs would carry her down the wide, white beach. She flung her arms out, and her hair flew back behind her bright eyes and ruddy cheeks in a breathtaking, glorious way. Suddenly she found a loud squeal bursting from her lips. She twirled around in a circle, murmuring over and over to herself, "Land! land! 'Tis *truly* land!"

Suddenly she tumbled down into a thicket of tall grass. She breathed in deeply, smelling the sharp earthy scent and taking in gasping breaths, choking down the smells she had hungered for while on the long, long Atlantic crossing. For a while she lay there, hearing the other children's frantic, joyous shrieks on the beach and resting in the solitude of the waving grasses until a voice said quietly at her side, "John has spotted a flock of geese."

She jumped and turned, spotting Joshua, who said in a low voice, "Hush now, and come along if you wish to watch."

Hope did not know if she cared to watch John kill the fowl, but curiosity overcame her fear and disgust. She followed Joshua softly from the grasses. Over and around a small bluff they walked, Hope trotting a little to keep up with Joshua's hurried strides, down to a secluded beach where John stood rigidly, watching a flock of birds quietly paddling around a pool surrounded by ocean rocks. Hope and Joshua stood behind John as he slowly raised the butt of the gun to his shoulder, squinting down the barrel. Hope covered her ears. *Bang!* The shot sounded, jolting John's body and echoing across the bare waters. The flock of geese flew up with a loud screech. Away they sailed through the winter sky, in a long *V* line, fleeing south.

"Did you kill one?" Hope demanded breathlessly, and John turned to her with a broad grin. "Look there." He pointed to the water where two limp bundles of feathers floated. Hope could have burst into tears as one of the poor geese gave a limp shudder before lying still, but Joshua seemed unfazed as he gave a loud whoop and dashed over the rocks, grasping one of the birds by the neck. "You got 'em both, John!" he cried excitedly. "We shall feast on fresh meat tonight!"

His words washed all disgust from Hope's mind, and she threw her arms in the air. "Fresh food!" she crowed. "Fresh meat!" She leapt on John's back, flinging her arms around his neck, and he laughed, spinning around. "Huzzah for John!" Hope cheered, and her stomach began to rumble.

Upon reaching the shores of Cape Cod, the men dared not attempt the sailing further south for several reasons—the largest one being the rapidly approaching winter months, which then yielded the need to build shelters for themselves as quickly as possible.

After choosing to begin searching for appropriate land near Cape Cod, they found it necessary to at once write up the standards of law to the best of their ability at that point and time. The debates about the document rose up for nearly a week, giving an impatient Hope the most trying time. There were hotly opposing sides, but at last John—who was Hope's chief informer on the political matters that she knew so little about—declared to her that the document was written, approved, and would do very well until other such things could be stamped more strongly into the plantation of the land. "Shall I read it to you?" he asked her, as her finger softly stroked the crinkled paper with swirls of ink that rose and fell in curves and curlicues over the surface of the copy

Father had shown Mother. She shrugged, and he began. "In the name of God, Amen. We, whose names are underwritten, the Loyal Subjects of our dread sovereign Lord, King James, by the Grace of God, of England, France, and Ireland, King, Defender of the Faith, et cetera,

"Having undertaken for the Glory of God, and Advancement of the Christian Faith, and the Honour of our King and Country, a voyage to plant the first colony in the northern parts of Virginia; do by these presents, solemnly and mutually in the Presence of God and one of another, covenant and combine ourselves together in a civil Body Politick, for our better Ordering and Preservation, and Furtherance of the Ends aforesaid; And by Virtue hereof to enact, constitute, and frame, such just and equal Laws, Ordinances, Acts, Constitutions, and Offices, from time to time, as shall be thought most meet and convenient for the General good of the Colony; unto which we promise all due submission and obedience.

"In witness whereof we have hereunto subscribed our names at Cape Cod the eleventh of November, in the Reign of our Sovereign Lord, King James of England, France and Ireland, the eighteenth, and of Scotland the fifty-fourth. Anno Domini, 1620."

Hope gazed at the page in wonderment. "Is that our government?" she asked with some astonishment.

John nodded and touched the paper with a reverent expression. "We are to live by it accordingly until we are able to create a true government—strong, free, firm, and fair." He took a deep breath, his face flushed with emotion. "God forbid this land ever become bondage under the slavery of unnecessary regulations that hamper a man's rightful freedoms. God forbid it."

A squalling flock of geese flew south as Hope gazed out toward the land, her cloak wrapped tightly around her. Winter was drawing near. For that reason being, the men were setting out that very day to scour the land in search of a place to build their plantation. The shallop had already been lowered into the water, and in a few minutes they would set off.

"Shan't you say farewell?"

It was a familiar teasing voice behind her, and she turned. Her chilled face caused John to look at her sharply. "Are you quite alright, Hope?" he asked in concern.

"*I* am fine," she answered slowly, gazing toward Father as he shouldered his musket and conversed with a stout man, Myles Standish. She looked back at John. "But will you be?"

John's concern cleared, and he smiled. "We will both be fine, little sister." His voice was lined with confidence, causing Hope's fears to subside slightly. He grinned and opened his arms, and she ran into them as he gave her a tight embrace. "Be good to Mother, now," he whispered in her ear, then winked as he hurried off to join Father.

Hope waved as he climbed nimbly down the rope ladder to the shallop below, disappearing from sight. Then she sighed. The cold wind was picking up, so she hurried down to the 'tween deck.

The next three days were spent in its dreariness. The misery felt on the ship lengthened considerably without John there to console and entertain her. Loneliness swept over often, for she soon found that the ship became dull without the liveliness he and Joshua managed to stir up often. The drab 'tween deck grew more and more drab and damp and cold, as Hope began to slip into a dull-witted state during the dark hours spent watching the days inch slowly by.

One day, however, she received a reckless awakening.

She sat on her hammock, leaning her chin on her fist and wondering what John was doing at that very moment. She felt an ache in her chest as she began to miss his easy presence, when suddenly her eardrums split. She thought she saw a flash of bright light from somewhere before she was flung to the floor as an explosion hurled the ship in a blinding state of wild rocking, knocking Hope against the side and sending penetrating screams spinning in the air. The *Mayflower* slowed its violent motion, but the screams remained pinned; suddenly she realized it was she who was screaming, and it was then that, in place of the shrieks, tears took place and ran down her cheeks freely. "What was it?" she sobbed, her mind now alive from utter fear. "Oh, what was it?"

Her eyes were so blurred she did not see the stormy sailor come bursting down into the 'tween deck, dragging a much frightened boy by the ear and confronting his parents with a furious tongue.

At length, Mother approached her with a pale face and told her what had happened. "Francis Billington was in the powder room," she said tightly. "He thought it an amusing joke to set off one of the guns to frighten us. Dangerous it may be, but 'twas not nearly as dangerous as it turned out, for the foolish, careless lad had spilled powder on the floor as well. He lit the gun *in* the powder room. Foolishness is not strong enough to describe his deeds, Hope, for had that flame, had one *spark* landed on the kegs of gunpowder, we should have been shattered to pieces."

Hope's hand flew involuntarily to her chest, her heart throbbing. The tears remained flowing steadily down her cheeks as Mother went on. "The gun went off, and the powder so carelessly having been strewn across the floor flew up in flames in one instant before disappearing completely." She paused a moment before saying, "'Tis a miracle we are still alive—alive and sound."

She looked at Hope. She sat trembling, and her dark hair clung pitifully to the tears that stained her cheeks. Mother's thin face tightened, and after giving her daughter's shoulders a quick squeeze, she slipped away, leaving Hope to blindly grasp a rough blanket nearby and bury her face in it. Her chest heaved as the tears streamed down, and she choked, trying to fight off the terrifying thoughts. Death had come far too close in those few instances. She shuddered and hugged the blanket, now balled up in a queer bundle, and leaned against the side of the ship. Her nervous mind allowed little focus, but deep down the longing was burning freely. Father and John must come home soon. She gasped, muttering the words aloud before drifting off to sleep.

"Hope."

The voice whispered near her ear, and she felt strangely calmed by the familiarity of it. Her eyelids flew open a moment later, and she gave a joyful shriek as she saw John crouched next to her, sitting back on his heels. He laughed as she flung her arms around his neck, though he seemed a bit puzzled by the earnestness in which she did so, for it was a sort of desperate, anxious earnestness that he remained confused over until she told him of the recent happenings aboard ship. His brown eyes widened in astonishment over Francis' now infamous achievement, and at long last, when Hope had completed her tale with a pale face, he said with a forced smile, "Well then, I suppose he accomplished what he had set out to do. He utterly and completely frightened everyone."

Hope looked at him drily, but he merely tousled her hair and began an account of the happenings of his group scouring the land. It was so intriguing that Hope quite forgot her other troubles aboard ship until he finished with the statement, "We did not find a place to settle, so we are setting out again tomorrow."

She froze, her eyes widening. "John, you said 'twould take little time to find a place! You said—"

John held up his hand to stop her before sighing, "I know, Hope, but I had not realized how difficult 'twould be to find the area perfect for our plantation. I would come nigh saying that there is far *too* much land out there if it did not fill one with such utter freedom—if it did not make one feel so desperately alive that you know not whether to shout or sing or simply fall on your knees drinking in the awesome earth. Ah, but 'tis hard to sift out all the spots to the right one. There is quite enough land out there. And we shall not stop scouring it until paths be wrought among the acres of wilderness."

Hope was quiet. Finally she asked softly, "But shall it be completed in time?"

John looked at her suddenly, his lips pressed tightly together. "You perceive far too much, Hope."

Hope's heart tightened, but she shrugged.

John sighed. "The winter is fast approaching, to be sure. We are doing the best we can, Hope. You can be certain of that."

Hope hugged her chest dejectedly. "The food is growing scantier and scantier each day," she mentioned softly, gazing about the crowded 'tween deck. "I daren't wonder how long it will last." She looked at him.

He was looking down at his hands, a hesitant look on his face. "Hope, suppose I told you that I left out a bit of my tale."

Her eyes widened. "How do you mean?"

"Suppose I told you we brought back provisions."

Hope's face broke into a grin. "Did you kill a grouse?"

"No, nothing of that sort. 'Tis corn, Hope. We found it buried beneath a deserted Indian structure."

Hope froze. "Indian structure?"

"I did mention it was deserted. However, I left out more to my tale." He stopped a moment, considering, before saying slowly, "I think it shall suffice to say that there *are* Indians in this land."

Hope searched his face, but he was gazing at the floor. "Were they threatening?" she probed, anxiety gnawing at her throat. "Were you quite safe?" Her voice began to rise involuntarily.

John held up his hands. "Hope, calm yourself. I am here, if you have not noticed. We do have weapons."

"They attacked?"

"Indeed, but we are safe, and they are safe. They were presumably frightened. After all, this is their land, and we are invading it, though we hope to befriend them and live in peace. We are safe and well, for the moment, however, and I am not so very worried about them. 'Tis this bitter cold that troubles me." He shivered and leaned against the wall, his brow furrowed in thought.

Hope sighed and fell back on her hammock. "When shall you be back?" she asked presently.

He straightened then, saying firmly, "We shall be back when we find the perfect place to build."

CHAPTER XV

Confidences

Hope strained her eyes for a sight of the land ahead, but the spray of murky sea water dashing against the side of the shallop was relentless and would not so much as let a glimpse penetrate the misty wall. Hope sighed and sat back again, squirming partly from excitement and partly from the frigid breeze blowing through the air. "When shall we be there?" she asked John impatiently.

He laughed and tousled her hair. "Soon enough."

She sighed once more and pulled her knitted cloak closer around her shoulders. Her jaw, clenched to keep her teeth from chattering, became wearied, and she shivered again. John draped his arm over her shoulder, saying with brotherly jest, "Cold?"

Hope tossed him a scornful look, and he immediately assumed an innocent air, saying, "Why, what did I say?"

She gave him a little shove, declaring, "You are the most impish fellow I daresay I have ever known!"

Joshua shot her a glance with an injured look on his

face, so Hope said comfortingly, "You are a close second."

Peals of carefree laughter followed, partly from the ridiculous banter and partly from the rising excitement within all of them. Home was just around the bend—or what was supposed to be home. Hope felt rebellion rising up within her once again at the thought of this wild land ever becoming her home, but she decided to make no mention of it at the moment, for such days of excitement should not be interrupted with unwanted feelings.

Suddenly Hope felt a distinct bump. The shallop bounced a few times as it gently landed by a large rock on shore; soon a few men leapt out, securing the boat to a branch jammed into the ground. She stepped out and gazed about the land, dreary with winter showing its face from the bare woods, to the cold beach, to the patches of snow on the land.

A hand touched her shoulder, and she turned to see John smiling fondly down on her as he beckoned her to follow him. He led her up a hill, cleared of trees and covered with browning grass. Up and up they strode, while the other people still milled about at the foot of the slope.

At long last John stopped. They stood upon the hill, near the edge of the wood, but far enough from the tree-lined depths to get a glimpse of the bay down below.

"Here." It was the only word John needed to say. Hope understood. She looked down at the starkly dry and drab grass beneath her feet and knew that very soon it would serve as the floor to their new home.

She took in a deep breath of the crisp winter air. A hint of snow was mixed in with the tingling cold that scalded her nose. She looked up at the sky, as if expecting a gray cloud to be in sight, but it was perfectly clear. Brilliant blue spread across the entire atmosphere above her, as if the cheerfulness of Spring and Autumn would not hide themselves even during Winter.

"Does it not hint of God's majesty?" John murmured next to her, gazing up at the flawless sky.

Hope felt a pang in her chest. "I suppose," she murmured, but her mind was elsewhere. She was thinking of the faith that John so steadfastly clung to and how she could not grasp it though she tried. She twisted her hands together in effort to hold back the anxieties that began grinding the edges of her heart, but they plundered in uninvited. Strong, nameless fears settled darkly over her, and she felt panic—a familiar feeling she had grown to despise—begin to rise in her throat. Finally she cried out, "John!"

He glanced at her, and she found herself groping for words. At length, she whispered, "What if Spring does not come?"

John's brown eyes stared deeply into hers until she felt he was seeing straight into her heart, and his expression was so calm that she became desperate to understand the queer peace that was ever etched across his face. At length, he said, "We have hope, little sister. It brightens the dark winter days and brings forth the vision of starting this new, beautiful plantation. It gives faith its foothold; it put forth root when Christ rose from the grave. Spring will come."

"But how are you so utterly sure?" Hope persisted, her heart aching. "How do you know hope is real? How can you cling to something that you cannot see?"

John knitted his eyebrows together. At length, he knelt next to her and pointed to the yellow sun glinting in the sky. "We can be sure as we know the sun will rise," he said softly. "Every evening it sets, bringing upon the darkness of night. But you know it will come again, do you not? It always returns, defeating the evils of nighttime and crushing the nightmares that haunt the dark."

Hope bit her lip, feeling tears fill her eyes.

"And hope is like the hint of its forthcoming. The stars penetrate through the dark sky, glistening and enlightening the soul that will search for them. We cannot see the evidence ahead of us, straining our eyes into the future. We must look above to see the shining hints that tell of the marvelous things to come after the weight of the dark night."

Hope choked. "And suppose clouds come hide the hopes above?"

He looked up at her. Somehow she was unsurprised to see tears trembling in his eyes. "Then one must have faith," he whispered, and she said no more. She looked away as a choking sensation rose in her throat. Somehow she felt in one single moment that the peace John had portrayed to her had desicively swept away from her reach.

Hope fiddled impatiently as she swung back and forth on her hammock in the 'tween deck. It was chilly outside the brazier's halo of warmth, but Hope was too agitated to care. The construction of the plantation began that very day, and she was *not* pleased. She dug her heel into the floor and pushed herself so far back that she accidentally knocked the breath out of herself as she slammed into the wall. She crossed her arms over her chest and scowled, refusing to reveal the panic welling up inside of herself as her breath would not return.

As she was struggling to breathe, Patience Danford approached her, saying arrogantly, "Why, Hope Ellison, 'tis a wonder you would sit still after wrestling with yourself ever since this morning."

At that precise moment, Hope's breath came back to her in a huff, and she gave a few queer gasps that rather frightened the red-headed girl before her, though Patience made no sign of shock—excepting it was quite plainly noted that her freckles stood out alarmingly as her face paled to a lighter color than usual. "Well, Patience," Hope, after recovering, said calmly, though attitude pierced her tone, "I suppose that the date does not trouble you in the least."

Patience stood for a moment, glaring perpetually. Finally she said haltingly, "How—do you—mean?"

"To-day is December twenty-fifth."

Patience's dark eyes widened as she asked in surprise, "*Is* it?" Then suddenly she remembered her dignity and lifted her chin abruptly.

"It is." Hope swung back and forth again, her dark eyebrows knitted together in anger. "And no one shall celebrate. 'Twas stated this morning, do you not remember? Oh, dear me, I had entirely forgotten. You were sleeping, poor girl. Is your headache gone now, dear?" The latter sentences were nearly smothered in taunting sarcasm. Patience seemed almost ready to fly into a frazzle then and there, but she instead clutched her red hair—as she was wont to do in dire situations—and said in a fiery tone, "I had thought it was, but your *soothing* remarks have hastened its return." She brushed her forehead in a way in which Hope privately thought to be much too melodramatic, and flounced away, caring little that it be Christmastide or not.

Hope scowled and fiercely flung back the hammock in which she was sitting. She found herself lying on the floor and seeing stars a moment afterward. She groaned and stood, preparing herself to plead with Mother on why they could not celebrate the least bit.

Her mouth watered as she remembered the scrumptious gingerbread she had feasted on last year. Her elders did not believe in celebrating the holiday in such worldly ways, but Mother still had filled the table with an unusual amount of food, much to Father's displeasure. It had become a tradition, and though Father did not appear to approve, it was quite impossible not to notice the heaping amounts of chicken, plum pudding, and cornbread he devoured, and Hope was convinced he enjoyed every minute of it.

She spotted Mother stirring broth in an iron kettle sitting on one of the braziers. "Mother," she said in a wheedling tone, "can we not celebrate Christmastide the least bit this year?"

"Hope," she gasped, nearly dropping the ladle into the kettle. "Do not say such things." She glanced around anxiously before bending toward Hope and repeating in a sharp whisper, "Do not say such things, Hope Ellison. 'Tisn't proper, nor agreeable to our convictions." She straightened and went back to stirring the distasteful broth. She glanced at Hope a moment, hesitating, before saying quietly, "Rose Standish is dreadfully ill, Hope, and I fear that the cold is taking its toll on the poor woman. We musn't think of the things we haven't and be grateful for the things we have this Christmastide."

Hope started and looked at Mother with wide eyes. "How ill?"

Cry of Hope

"Very," was Mother's short answer, but from the tightness of her face, Hope knew that "very" was an understatement. She looked toward the corner of the ship, where Rose Standish lay on her hammock. Every now and then a cough followed by a hacking, gasping sound would send the bed in tremors, revealing a pale, thin woman—nearly transparent—with dark sunken eyes in the middle of her face. Her once soft, dark hair was now stringy with sweat and clinging to her hot, feverish face. Hope shuddered and turned away, but she could not return to her place before with the same ironic pleasure of complaining. She attempted to sit, but it felt so cold and barren and hollow that she stood quickly, nearly cracking her head on a low support. She bound toward the ladder and scrambled upon deck.

The sky was full of white, churning clouds. The blasts of frigid wind that seared though Hope's thin cloak sent shivers through her body, but she attempted to ignore it by squinting to see the land where the men were building ahead of her. She could barely make out a few shadows moving back and forth, but the howling wind and hazy air made it far too difficult to see clearly. She sighed, resting her forearm dejectedly on the rail as she toyed mindlessly with a splinter clinging to the rough wood. Her eyes darted toward the sky, and she wondered how soon the men would return from work. It was pale white, but Hope was sharp enough to notice a brighter whiteness toward the west, and she knew that in a few hours they would return. "Foolish winter," she muttered. "If it were not for you, I could spend my days happily watching on land. As it is, you are already condemning Rose Standish with illness." She frowned and leaned her head on her arm, closing her eyes to the blinding wind.

Suddenly she felt something settle softly on her cold cheek; then it landed with a sharp sting on her eyelid. She gasped and glanced quickly upward. Something cold fell into her eye. She blinked, glancing around. Opening up her palm, she watched as a tiny white flake settled peacefully on it before diminishing as her warm hand melted it into a tiny droplet. A gust of wind sent it flying, and Hope gazed around her in awe as soft, heavy white crystals floated down in an endearing winter enchantment. "How *lovely!*" she cried and spun around among the dancing snowflakes, feeling like a winter princess if there were such a thing. Her cloak flew out behind her, flapping in the wind, and she tilted back her ruddy cheeks with a bright smile, saying, "I suppose there *are* some pleasant things in winter after all!"

CHAPTER XVI
Trifling Predicaments and Serious Problems

Hope huddled in front of the brazier, attempting to warm her aching hands. She sipped from a mug filled with hot broth and sighed as it slipped down her throat, warming her chest. *John should be back soon,* she thought as she pushed back her hair, wet with melting snow.

No sooner had the words entered her head than did the hatch fling open and the men troop in, tools in hand and faces ruddy from cold. Hope smiled as she took another sip of her broth, and soon, as she expected, John emerged from the crowd with Joshua and sat next to Hope. "Ah!" he cried gratefully, holding his hands close above the brazier, while Hope set her finished mug down at her feet and sat with her arms wrapped around her knees, watching his face with sparkling eyes. "How did work go?" she ventured after a moment, unable to wait until her brother announced the news to her.

"Very well," John replied between teeth clenched from cold. "Felling trees during a snowstorm, however, is quite bothersome."

Joshua let out a hearty laugh. "'Tis, but the work keeps us warm," he told Hope with a smile.

"What have you accomplished to-day?" she asked, attempting to hide her impatience and feeling as if she did well, though in truth she failed utterly. John grinned, and Joshua replied with twinkling eyes, "We felled trees."

"Oh." Hope could not hide her disappointment this time, and she asked dully, "When shall the plantation be completed?"

John gazed into the fire, rubbing his arms. "I would prefer not to predict. 'Twill take quite some time, to say the least."

Hope looked down at her shoes. "Oh."

"In the meantime," Joshua flashed her a mischievous smile, "you can busy yourself making scrumptious pottage for us. Perchance there is some of such to eat now? I feel half-starved."

Hope smiled, standing up. "Shall I fetch you both a mugful?"

"Indeed? I am most grateful." Joshua nodded teasingly.

John hesitated, looking away. Shaking his head, he rubbed his arms with a grimace. "I am not hungry, little sister. I would rather warm up a bit."

Hope glanced at him anxiously. "What is wrong?"

He shrugged.

Hope looked at him closely. His soft eyes were glazed over just the slightest, giving her heart a sudden skip of fear.

"Are you alright?" she asked, slipping close to him.

He laughed, shaking his head of dark hair. He looked at her fondly. "I am quite myself, Hope. I am merely tired, and the cold gives my head an ache."

Hope sighed, crossing her arms over her chest. "I wish the plantation were completed now. Then you needn't work in such hampering weather."

"We will finish it by and by," John said softly. He gazed into the brazier. "That is why we work day after day. One step at a time matters more than one would think."

Silence followed. Hope slipped her small arm around John's shoulders, and he smiled at her reassuringly, settling her fears with one caring glance.

The next morning Hope awakened, utterly oblivious to the workload she would find placed on her shoulders that day due to disheartening discoveries. Out of her hammock she went, slipping into her heavy black shoes, draping her blanket over her shoulders, and wrapping it around herself. Lately she had been sleeping in her cloak at nights, as well as her wool dress, for the air drew colder and colder in and around the dark corners of the ship, steadily creeping nearer to the golden halo around the braziers. This morning Hope was uncontrollably shivering as the air seeped through the blanket, cloak, dress, and underthings, scalding her bare skin underneath and nipping the very marrows of her bones.

She slipped into the warm circle around one of the braziers and held her chapped hands above it, watching the small dancing flame inside. John and the men must have left already, she reasoned as she glanced about the room. She frowned, realizing how still it was, and began to wonder if she had awoken earlier than usual. But she soon found she had not, for a young woman, Priscilla, approached her, asking if she might make the stew to-day. "I am sorry, Hope," she said desperately as her hand went up to push back a strand of hair from her forehead. "My mother is ill, and two of the men could not rise this morning due to fever."

Hope looked at her with wide eyes, her heart thumping. "Fever?" she asked anxiously, and Priscilla's sad eyes answered her inquiry. Hope's voice seemed to be lost a moment before she said numbly, "I will make the pottage."

She glanced around for Mother, for she was well aware of her incapability to take upon an important task such as making of the pottage. But she spotted her tending to Rose Standish, and she dared not trouble her. Instead, she fought to remember the requirements and took the burden upon her own shoulders. She thought it rather good of her until she accidentally dropped hardtack into the pottage. She glanced around quickly to see if anyone had spotted her mistake, and as everyone appeared to be oblivious, she gingerly fished up the nasty things with the ladle and dumped them back in the barrel.

After that mistake, she considered again of approaching Mother for help. But as her eyes scanned the 'tween deck, she caught sight of the still, feverish forms on the hammocks, and a sudden conscious awareness came upon her. Just the day before those men had been working strongly on the plantation, and now they were battling a frightful fever raging throughout their veins. She froze as such thoughts crossed her head. A hideous awe overcame her, filling her heart with such dark fears that had she not given herself a terrible shake and returned to her work, she may have fallen into a fit of hysterics.

By noon the soup was completed, and Hope kept watch of it throughout the afternoon, stirring the pottage every few minutes as seemed proper. But during the long, lonely hours that day, she could not help fearing the next few minutes. Would another voyager fall ill? What would become of them?

It was as she sat with her forehead resting on her fist that she heard the commotion near the back of the 'tween deck. She started and looked up quickly, her heart pounding in her throat.

Mother, who had been tending to Rose Standish, stood back a few feet from the hammock, her hand flung to her mouth and her eyes alarmingly wild. Hope leapt to her feet as she saw Priscilla hurry over to examine Rose. Her jaw dropped as Priscilla paled and gently positioned Rose's limp hands over her chest before stepping back, her fists gripping the folds of her apron.

"Oh, poor Captain Standish!" a gasp could be heard. Grieved tears began around the room, and Hope's heart began to thump so sharply against her ribs that she could not bear it. She flew up deck, away from the contaminated 'tween deck, and away from the presence of Death that had slunk in unwanted. She gasped as she burst into the cold and flung herself toward the rail, burying her face in her shaking arms as her back heaved. She was not left to her fearful sobbing long, for she heard the clatter of the men returning. As she looked up from the warmth of her arms, the tears froze mercilessly on her cheeks. She spotted John boarding the *Mayflower*, rubbing his arms and chuckling as Joshua appeared to be immersed in conversation with him, but as her brother glanced around deck, he spotted Hope's disheveled figure and frowned.

"Hope!" he cried as he saw her. "What are you doing out in this freezing cold?"

Hope gasped, and he hurried to slip an arm around her shoulder, bending to look concernedly into her eyes. "Hope, what is wrong?"

"Rose Standish," she whispered, "Rose Standish is... is dead."

John's eyes widened, and he slowly stood, drawing her under his cloak. "'Twill be alright, little sister," he whispered uncertainly, but at that moment another commotion was heard as Myles Standish hurled himself toward the rail, slamming his trembling fist on the splintered wood. His back began to heave. Hope caught the bitter glint of anguished tears that rolled down his red cheeks, and she could not face it any longer. She buried her face in John's cloak and wept.

CHAPTER XVII
Stern Impassioned Stress

"Is the pottage nearly finished, Hope?" a tired voice asked.

It was late. The men hadn't returned from the burial. Mother had vanished from sight. Hope lay shivering on her hammock, staring blankly at the ceiling.

At the word of the pottage, however, a short squeal escaped her lips. She leapt to her feet and darted toward the kettle, catching up a ladle to stir it before it was spoilt. She was too late. It had scorched, and Hope slumped down on a barrel. *I am a hopeless homemaker,* she thought bitterly, just as the hatch flew open, and a burst of cold air entered the 'tween deck.

Before she could think of a thing to cover up her mistake and appease the weary-worn men, John emerged from the crowd and sat down heavily on a barrel, exhaustion filling his countenance. Concern washed all thoughts of the pottage from her mind, and she approached him at once. She touched his shoulder. He looked up, his face grim.

"Did it go very badly?" she murmured, absentmindedly

clutching the ladle in her hand.

"It went as well as expected," he replied, stretching his legs out toward the brazier with a wince.

Joshua appeared a moment later. He, too, looked grimmer than usual, but he managed to say cheerfully, "I suppose we have pottage again? I am quite famished."

Hope choked, holding the ladle out to him. "I am afraid I spoilt it," she whispered. "I managed to forget about it, and it scorched."

She was surprised by a sudden chortle from John. She looked at him. He was grinning up at her, the relief of merriment in his eyes. "You truly spoilt it?" he asked incredulously.

Hope nodded miserably.

Joshua laughed. "I shall fetch some of such spoilt pottage and taste it for myself. Shall I fetch you some, comrade?"

John hesitated. He stretched his arms out and grimaced, finally saying, "I do not feel hungry in the least, Joshua."

Hope glanced sharply at him.

He caught her fearful expression, and though she tried to hide it, he must also have caught the disappointment in her eyes, for he said to his friend, "Rather, I think I shall *taste* Hope's pottage. After all, 'tis the first she has ever made on her own."

"A momentous occasion, indeed." Joshua nodded with a grin and left.

Hope looked at her brother. He had leaned his head back against the support behind the barrel, gazing up at the low ceiling with an expression of intent thoughtfulness. Hope watched him a moment until his face suddenly cleared, and he glanced at her. "What is wrong, little sister?" he asked fondly.

Hope shrugged and changed the subject by saying dejectedly, "I am a wretched homemaker."

John smiled. "No. You haven't much practice. That is all."

Just then Joshua returned with mugs brimming with pottage, and so ended the conversation. He handed one to John, wrapping his chapped hands around the other. "It certainly *smells* scorched, but that does not determine the taste." He winked at Hope.

Hope gave him a half-smile. His expression didn't change as he took a sip, but it was a moment before he said stolidly, "It tastes scorched."

"What? Surely not," John cried teasingly, and he sipped from his mug. His face contorted. "Yes, comrade," he nodded, licking his lips. "'Tis most assuredly scorched."

Hope frowned darkly, disappointed in herself.

John smiled. "But 'tis the best scorched pottage I have yet tasted."

"I intend on eating it," Joshua said stoutly. "After all, I did say I was famished."

"In other words, you shall eat it as there is nothing else," Hope finished.

Joshua nodded slowly. "More or less, yes." And he grinned quite contagiously.

However, after a brief moment of cheerfulness, the hatch to the 'tween deck was flung open. A gust of cutting winter air whirled angrily in, and slowly a hunched figure stumped down the ladder. Hope involuntarily grabbed John's arm. His jaw was trembling.

The figure turned, revealing a pair of haggard bloodshot eyes. A sudden pang shot through Hope's heart as she recognized Captain Standish. His usual red, cheerful face had vanished into the winter storm that was quickly shrouding them all in gloom, and from then onward, Hope's fears dared not leave her again.

Hope huddled by the brazier. The air in the 'tween deck seemed to have frozen. She shuddered as her eyes darted from one hot, perspiring face to the next. Their fevers would break, of course, she tried to assure herself. But the still white form of Rose Standish stood out vividly in her mind, and she could not escape the fear.

A thump from above startled her out of her busy reverie, and she looked up at the low ceiling in surprise, wondering why the men were back so early. She glanced toward Mother, who was staring at the hatch that suddenly flew open. Winter air shrieked into the confines of the 'tween deck. Hope blinked as the wind stung her eyes, and when she looked again at Mother, her stomach dropped. Her face had turned white.

Hope felt a wave of nausea wash over her, and she turned sharply toward the ladder. A shrill scream burst from her lips.

A perspiring, pale face was watching her out of hollow brown eyes. John's form was leaning heavily on Joshua's shoulder, and his lips moved, as if trying to speak. Suddenly his eyes rolled back into his head, and he crumpled to the floor. Commotion began wildly around Hope, but she did not know it. Her eyes burned into John's heaving back, and her head reeled as she gasped, "No!" The room swam before her, careening until it finally crumbled into an ash-like darkness.

Never before had Hope awakened with such a passion of fear storming inside of her. She barely noticed the cold floor she tread, nor the icy air that bit her lungs. No, 'twas a fear that shut out everything but the cause of the ignition, and she fled to her brother's bedside the instant she awoke from her unconsciousness.

His chest rose and fell, grasping every bit of air his weak lungs could muster. Hope trembled as she approached him, collapsing to her knees by his hammock. "John!" she gasped, reaching out to grip his hand. "John!" But the fever raged so severely throughout his veins that his brain had snapped from coherency into an unrecognizable delirium. Hope's face was a stranger's to him. She paled alarmingly at the emptiness in which he gazed at her, his brown eyes hollow with the flask of fever forced down his throat.

"Hope, go."

She turned, her eyes blurred with tears of hysteric, and she laid her head on Mother's lap, deriving comfort from the source she least desired it from.

But Mother lifted Hope's chin with her finger, saying in a whisper, "Leave this isle of fever, daughter. Leave now. Remain in your hammock until I bid you to return."

"No!" Hope wrenched away, lying her cheek against John's motionless hand.

A heavy step was heard, and she found herself gazing

up into Father's haggard face. "Have you heard your mother?" he demanded huskily, taking her shoulders and dragging her to her feet. "Return to your hammock."

At that moment, something ruptured within Hope. Rage shot throughout her veins, and she recoiled, clutching a splintered support. She breathed heavily, spitting fire into her father's eyes. Finally she gasped, "You ought to have listened to him."

He paled.

Hope felt an icy chill singe her spine.

Then Father shrank into the shadows.

Hope's trembling hands weakly grasped the support, but she was unable to hold herself upright. She stumbled to John's bedside and heeded not Mother's silent weeping. She took her brother's hand in her own and squeezed it. Then she plummeted into the blackness of dreamland.

Nightmares swallowed her the moment she drifted into that deep, restless sleep. They slunk in the dark, sneering, drooling, and capturing Hope, drawing her into heinous mirages that came and disappeared with every breath. When she awoke, she found herself in a worse state of exhaustion than before. She looked into her brother's still face, his forehead lined with perspiration. Then she broke into tears.

A jerky breath hacked helplessly from John's swollen throat, sending a spasm of fright through Hope's body. A trickle of blood stained his chin, and she felt a quake of fear run down her spine. She found herself cowering from the danger that lurked within her beloved brother, and her hand trembled as she touched his cracked knuckles. "Do not leave," she whispered tremulously, brushing her cheek against his motionless fingers. "Please do not leave me."

The tears rained down her cheeks, and she buried her face in John's hand and wept.

Howling wind scurried around the corners of the ship. Hope awoke shuddering, wondering what was weighing so heavily on her heart that it pounded uncontrollably. She rolled over, squeezing her eyes shut and feeling she would rather not remember what brought upon such fearful anxiety. But despite her efforts to hold it back, the recollection came back in a rush.

John was ill.

Her eyelids flew open, and she started so violently that the hammock overturned, sending her in a sprawling heap upon the frigid floor. She gasped, scrambling to her feet, and stumbled toward John's bedside in a daze. "How is he?" she whimpered, staring at his pale face.

Mother shook her head, her chin trembling.

Hope covered her face with her hands.

Suddenly a gentle palm rested on her shoulder, and she turned. Joshua's eyes were filled with shameless tears as he looked upon the ill form of his comrade. Hope shook with pain.

She scarcely noticed when he slipped away, but a moment later she recognized the fact that she was again alone. Slipping to take her place by John's bedside, she could not force out the dry tears that protruded the mask concealing her heart. Instead, she gazed agonizingly at her brother's still form.

"Oh!" It was a gasp that escaped her lips, and she hid her eyes with cold fingers. She had suddenly envisioned his motionless frame horrifyingly similar to Rose Standish's silent one, and she knew she could not bear such a picture.

"No!" she mumbled into her hand that was clasped over her mouth. The words grew fiercer, sharper, as they shrieked shrilly throughout her mind. She pressed her fists against her temples in torment, muttering, "You *cannot!* You *shall* not!" She felt her pulsing heart beat against the harsh cold of her fingertips, and she squeezed her eyes shut, blocking out the world. Time froze.

"Hope!"

It was a cry. She exploded from her soundless state, expecting an unbearable truth ready to steal her breath away.

But one sight softened the room around her. Her tensed fingers relaxed, and hot tears crept into her eyes. It was a familiar sight. A sight so sweet, so familiar that it hurt with a sharp, beautiful pain. She gazed into a pair of soft brown eyes, eyes she thought she might never again see in their original spirit. They were awake and perceptive with a depth of love, and she felt herself melt until she could no longer see. She buried her face in John's hammock. He made not a sound, but gently placed a hand on her head and stroked it with his old, undying fondness.

CHAPTER XVIII
Darkest Hour

The flickering light of the brazier illuminated Hope's face as she sat sipping broth that evening. She was acutely aware of her tumultuous appearance, but her weak state had reminded her of a more desperate need. With Mother's urgings, she had left John's bedside and taken a place by the warmth of the flame.

Now Mother joined her, and they sat together in silence. It felt peaceful, and Hope was overwhelmingly grateful for such a lull. The pottage tasted good, though it consisted only of water and corn. Hope breathed a sigh of contentment. "'Tis a relief," she said softly.

Mother said nothing in reply, but her face paled slightly at the words. Hope looked at her in concern.

At that moment, Priscilla approached with a mug of pottage, and she and Mother began conversing together as they ate. Hope grew weary of their talk, and during a brief moment of silence, she asked to be excused. Mother consented.

Hope slipped toward John's bedside. However, from

some feet away, she involuntarily paused, for she caught sight of Joshua seated next to her brother. John was speaking earnestly to him, and Hope felt this to be a very agreeable sight. *This shall be amusing*, she thought with a brief smile, for whenever the two boys were together, amusement of all kinds followed. She bounded forward to join them, saying with a bright smile, "What cheer, brother?"

Their conversation abruptly paused. John nodded silently at his friend.

Joshua stood hastily. Hope felt a jolt in her stomach as she caught sight of the startling tears trembling in his eyes. He brushed past, sending a look of penetrating compassion toward her for a brief instant. Then he disappeared into the shadows.

Hope stared in wonder at the place he had been, an incomprehensible air of fright suddenly consuming her.

"How do you fare, little sister?" John said, his voice husky.

Hope turned slowly toward him, studying his thin, pale face. His lips were upturned in a smile, but she saw the pain of sadness glinting in his eyes. She sat down quickly on a stool.

John was fast in catching the consternation written across her face, for he said soberly, "Come now, Hope..." Then he stopped.

Hope took a shaky breath, attempting to push back all of her fears, and said, "Come now, brother. Bid me to fetch you a mug of broth. I daresay it will send strength through you."

A flicker of a smile flashed across his face, and for a short moment, Hope spotted again the familiar light of buoyancy in his eyes. "No, indeed. I shall wait until the hunger begs it of me." His voice dropped, and the light vanished.

Hope felt the tremors of fear steal her heartbeat for a moment, and she closed her eyes to gain ground. Suddenly she felt a cold hand grasp her own, and her eyelids flickered open.

John gazed at her, a flame burning low in his eyes. "What is it you fear, little sister?" he asked in a hushed voice. "What is it you fear?"

Hope shook her head, her eyes blurring, and she looked away.

John was silent a moment. "You know," he said softly, a tear rolling down his cheek. "You know that, despite all the powers of fear, there will never be complete darkness. Hope will offer lights for us, if we never lose the faith that keeps it burning."

Hope looked down, sending a shower of droplets onto her dirty petticoat. She squeezed her brother's hand tightly, and he clung to hers. Finally she looked up and found him brushing away the tears that violently rolled down his cheeks. He gazed at her in the weak light, half-sitting up impulsively, and whispered, "You are my little sister, Hope Ellison. Yet, you shall not remain so little a girl much longer. You are growing into a great woman. Someday... oh, how I wish I could see..." His voice trailed off.

Hope was weeping. She blindly reached out her arms, and he enveloped her in an embrace. She clung to him and said into his ear, "I love you, brother."

She felt his tears stain her shoulder as he whispered back, "I love you more, little sister."

"Hope!"

She turned, brushing away the flakes of snow on her rosy cheeks. The evening sun barely penetrated the thick winter clouds as Priscilla appeared, breathing heavily.

Hope felt heat rise in her throat, and she said in a nearly inaudible voice, "What is it?"

"'Tis..." Priscilla paused, then grasped Hope's shoulders. "'Tis John."

Hope paled. "What is *wrong* with him?" she whispered, and a penetrating sense of dread welled up in her stomach.

"He is ill, Hope." Priscilla rubbed her eyes with exhaustion. "Worse than before," she moaned. But Hope had vanished, leaving a scatter of ice shards behind her.

Oh, John! Oh, John, John, no! she thought, gasping on the cutting air. She scrambled down the ladder, scraping her knuckles on the harsh wooden rungs. Hastily wiping her cheeks, she left a smear of red blood on her pale face, stinging her chapped skin.

She darted across the 'tween deck, blind to everything before her, and finally collapsed by John's bedside. She seized his cold hand in her own, burying her face in it. Her heart wrung within her chest, and with every painful beat, a rally of fears tore throughout her body. Spasms of emotion shook her, and she ached for the relief of tears.

At length a large hand abruptly wrenched her backward. She gasped as her head jolted back, and she tumbled upon the floor. Looking up wildly, she saw Father bending over his son, his face white. Feebly aware of

Mother's passionate wailing, she stood shakily on her feet and covered her face with her hands.

A moment later, she felt the presence of someone behind her. She looked up, expecting to find Priscilla's compassionate face, but instead looking into the eyes Joshua. He gazed at her brother with an agony-stricken countenance.

"He has so little strength left," he whispered at length in a tremulous voice.

Hope's throat tore at his words, and she gasped, "How can I fight for him?"

Joshua made no effort to respond, but a single tear rolled bitterly down his rough cheek. He wrapped an arm tightly around her shoulder. Groaning, she clutched his shirtsleeve and trembled, fear exploding wrathfully in her mind. The rawness of her heart singed with a sudden fury to fight her brother's battle, and she tore away from the refuge of empathy, dragging a stool by his bedside.

Her eyes met Father's, who stood across from her. A flash of pain and accusation collided in their gaze, and Father reeled back, a tempest of tears running down his face. He vanished from sight.

Groaning, Hope threw herself into battling John's fever and spent the remainder of the endlessly long evening flying about fetching fresh damp cloths, wetting his cracked lips, coaxing drops of water down his throat, and shedding tear droplets that often blemished the floor with bitter stains. Night slithered in without warning, and Hope found herself growing more and more exhausted, and fear tainted her healthy cheeks a sickly gray. She forbade herself to sleep, but her shoulders drooped. Her weary eyes closed involuntarily, sending her into an unwanted slumber. At once, she aroused herself, but she slipped off again, this time to spend several hours in the silent, dark world that offered relief from the anguish of her own.

She awoke sharply. Cursing the sleep she had so needed, her eyes darted toward John. She gasped. The starkly red cheeks and white deathlike face conflicted in a violent contrast that was ghastly to see. She whimpered, taking his cold hand in her own and rubbing it, hoping to instill some of the life from herself into his gray figure. But in vain it was, for he made still no movement. Indeed, he was so alarmingly silent that Hope grew paralyzed with fear. He gave a gruesome gasp, and Hope clutched his hand, nearly slicing it with her severe grip.

Suddenly he began writhing.

Hope leapt to her feet, her jaw dropping. Terror clutched her throat as she tried to scream. John twisted, sending the hammock into a fit and nearly upsetting the bed. A moan, grotesque and hoarse, drifted heavily from his lips, and Hope dropped his hand in utter fear. It flung out feebly, catching her ribs, but she paid no heed to it as she watched in horror the fierce red colour seeping from his cheeks. Suddenly, his writhing stopped. His hand, flung aimlessly in the air, dropped with a sickening hollow thud on the floor. Hope's heart split.

"*No!*" she shrieked, her throat exploding, and she flung herself by John's side, grasping his lifeless arm. She screamed, burying her face in his shoulder and clutching the thin hammock. Tremors shot throughout her pale form, and she tore at John's hand, smothering it with unforgiving tears. Thunderous footsteps clashed through her ears, and she found someone pulling her from her brother. She fought it, groping for his hand and clutching it fiercely; but they tore her from him, and she felt the world spinning around her as she collapsed on the hard floor, rolling into a ball and shrieking in anguish. Her eyes, blinded by perpetual tears, bore into her brother's still form. Suddenly she realized they were taking him. "Come back!" she moaned, her shaking fingers groping in the hazy air.

"Hope!" An arm clutched her shoulder, giving her a shake. "He's gone." She wept, her eyes rolling back into her head, as she tumbled into an endless, hopeless darkness.

CHAPTER XIX

Heartless

Fire burned in leaping yellow flames before her eyes. She twisted. Her lips cracked open, and she moaned. Suddenly she felt her insides heave as a dribble of frigid water slid down her throat. Her forehead felt swollen as heat seared across it in waves. When she attemped to brush it away, her arms fell to the ground, heavy and aching. She tried to speak, but a horrid blubbering noise betook her ears as soon as the words drifted from her numb lips, and she silenced, unable to bear such chilling sounds. Suddenly a numbing sensation overwhelmed her, and she drifted off into a black land. Unconscious.

    There were queer days that followed. Often she felt as if she might have awakened, but her crooked dreams appeared so similar to her contorted wakefulness that she never knew which was which. She felt, too, that her heart was darker and emptier than any she ever knew, though her mind, so dulled and twisted, could not place a finger on what caused it to feel in such a way. It was a vague melancholy that overtook her mind and body, unhealthy in form and heartrending in spirit.

She felt so miserable she did not send it on its way and so tired she did not bother to ask why it was there. She merely slept and woke and slept some more, tossing and turning with groans as her body felt on fire one moment and shivered with cold the next.

It was a moan that awoke her one morning. At first, she thought perhaps it was herself. She rubbed her swollen eyes and glanced beside her, finding a ghastly picture that nearly jumped her out of her nervous skin. A pair of dark eyes stared at her, but Hope knew they were unseeing. A face, paler than any Hope had seen, stood out starkly in the dark light. Indeed, Hope felt she should have seen the face before, but her groggy mind could not recall to whom it belonged. A moment later she gave a tremendous start, as she realized with shock that it was Patience Danford. She felt confusion and a sudden fear well over her as she wondered if perhaps something terribly wrong had happened while she was asleep.

Indeed, how long had she been asleep? She could not tell. She felt rather she had slept many, many days, but she was still tired—more tired than she had ever felt before.

She shoved back a stubborn lick of hair that insisted on catching in her wet eyelashes. *Were* they wet? Why were they wet?

Her hand suddenly clutched her stomach, and she whipped her head to the side, finding in strange surprise that she was retching. Why was she retching? Her stomach was not hurting. Or was it? She did not know. How could she know? She pressed her hand to her forehead, suddenly bursting into tears. Everything was so queer. Why was it so? She hiccuped.

Then abruptly she felt herself falling and entered

again a dream-world of utter blackness, with no other colour appearing excepting red: a fierce, sharp, burning red that refused to leave her side.

"Hope!"

It was a scream. It jolted her to her senses, and she flew up in bed, her blankets and cloak in a knotted tangle that nearly strangled her. She screamed, but a pair of hands clapped over her mouth. She struggled, yet they remained firm, while the mass of bed coverlets were gently removed from her sticky dress. A familiar voice spoke shakily, and Hope knew it was Mother.

Her mind suddenly lit up, and she blinked her eyes, feeling calmer. She knew it was Mother. She found herself glancing around the room. At first a strange mirage of glowing yellow colour kindled before her eyes, but then she caught sight of something glistening. She wiped a wet tear from her cheek, recognizing it to be the copper kettle.

Suddenly a queer picture flashed before her eyes. A familiar image it seemed, but hazy, until a hazel eye pierced through the cloud, and she recognized it at once to be Joshua.

But where was John? Surely he would come to her. He always did when he returned from work on the plantation.

Plantation? She felt a twinge in the back of her mind.

She felt a sudden awareness of a gentle swaying. The *Mayflower*...

Then her eyes widened. John. He was in the jumble somewhere. She began to search through her thoughts, her numb mind tingling as it began to whirl. Various images flashed before her eyes: a flashing explosion, her black shoes, mugs of scorched pottage. John. He had to be there—but where?

She began to feel frantic and grasped her forehead. John. Where was he? Her brother, the one whom she leaned upon. Her steady footing. Her shelter from the world. Had he disappeared? Her eyebrows knitted together, and her jaw was clenched so tightly it pained her. John. *Where had he gone?*

She froze. Gone. Indeed, he was gone. A myriad of pictures flashed before her eyes. His soft brown eyes. His sturdy, strong frame. His comforting presence. His long strides, his ringing laugh, his impish grin. His peaceful countenance. He was gone?

Her arms clutched her stomach, and she drew her knees up to her chest. Another picture arose in her mind, and she cringed. A face, violently red and white and deathly still, appeared. He was gone.

She gave a long, wailing gasp and abruptly froze. Her arms were coiled tightly around her legs, and her cheek was stuck fast to her knees. She would not face the dark world. She could not face the dark world. Her heart had torn in two, and it bled with more pain than she had feared it could. No light, no flickering burst of hue stood out in her mind; no, the world was dark. The world found pleasure in ripping every bright and secure hope that surrounded her, leaving her with nothing but a bitter, barren darkness. Her shelter had disappeared, and she was abandoned in the midst of a wild and lonely land, full of coarse whispers and taunting sneers, howling with a song of fear and melancholy that caused her very bones to shudder.

Such anger, feelings, pains, fears flew through head, but at last, after mulling over these thoughts in a jagged, confused way, she drifted off into a sleep once again, this time to last many days.

Hope was physically well. She had been taken with illness from shock and stress, but after a week, the fever left her, and her body could function once again. However, it was her mind that left her in a worse state than ever before. The jolt of losing her brother—the shock of losing her solid ground—had crushed her heart and mind, leaving her with a mass of confused emotions and utter anguish that cut into the minds of everyone who passed her.

Indeed, she rarely did anything, but sat on her hammock with her cloak wrapped around her shoulders while staring into space. Perhaps a passerby would think it tiresome or dull to sit in such a way for days on end, doing nothing but wallowing in grief. But indeed, Hope did not merely do nothing. The emotions that churned in her young chest surged with passionate zeal. With every beat of her heart, questions pounded into her head, each leaving in the same way, unanswered, and each adding another dose of anxiety to her burnt mind.

Eating was a thing of the past and was something she seldom took part in. It was only on occasion, when her stomach would suddenly pounce on her ribs, shaking her violently, that she recognized the fact that she was starving and must eat soon or die. Mother often pleaded with her, begging her to take a stroll, eat a hearty portion of stew, or help one of the fellow dying passengers. Hope instantly refused with a shake of her head and a look so haggard that Mother shuddered and turned away. The thought of seeing another ill, transparent or ghastly face caused Hope to tremble.

She seemed unaware, however, of her own appearance. Her eyes had sunk far back into her face and were rimmed by dark circles, which accentuated her green eyes, causing them to appear hollow and piercing. Her hair, so matted and tangled, was knotted at the back of her head, which in turn framed her face that grew steadily paler and thinner by each passing day. Indeed, she was a sight to behold, but the truth was she was not the only one with such melancholy features or worse. By mid-February it was clear that work on the plantation must pick up the pace before the entire congregation wasted away.

CHAPTER XX

Anguish

Lapping water rang in Hope's ears. She gazed down absently at her faded woolen cloak that had been constantly twisted tightly around her for many weeks. A vague remembrance crossed her mind. A rosy, smiling face had been before her when she had first tried that cloak on less than a year ago. She could still clearly hear the sunny laughter of Constance over some remark by... John? Yes, he had been there, leaning against the doorway. His roguish grin and twinkling brown eyes flashed before her memory, igniting a gush of tears that began to stream down her face, partially freezing in the winter wind. She shook, as memory over memory washed before her, and she found herself unable to stop.

"Cheer up, Hope," Mother said quietly by her side. "Moving to the common house should not be met with idle sobbing."

Hope would not cheer up. The rest of the ride in the shallop toward shore was spent in violent melancholy on her part.

Cry of *Hope*

Upon reaching shore, she glanced up the hill and saw the tip of the common house peeking above the trees that dotted the shoreline. She hastened out of the shallop, away from Mother and the crowd of voyagers. She scrambled along the worn pathway toward the newly completed building.

Along the way, she saw the skeletons of structures in the process of being built. The wind whistled through the thin clapboards tacked onto the beams and supports, sending her dizzily past with their eerie cry. Just ahead loomed the new shelter. The roof was freshly thatched with reeds, giving it a queer earthy look. The clapboards were unstained and looked worn from winter winds, for they were already dulled gray.

Hope wrinkled her nose and felt the cold tears still trickling off the tip of it. This was her home, she scoffed. To be shared with others she did not wish to be in the presence of at the moment. An overwhelming desire for privacy overcame her, and as she caught sight of the new villagers approaching between the tangle of bare tree limbs, she hastily darted off, vanishing into the thick forest.

Dodging branches and leaping over fallen logs, Hope ran. Her breath came in gasps, and her mind, though numb from loss, did recognize the foolishness of her actions. She had not heard of Indians of late.

She stopped in her tracks.

Indeed, she had paid little to no attention to the conversations of the men when they returned.

She froze, glancing around her. *Indians*. Perhaps they were watching her very movement. She had heard they seemed to be part of the woods themselves and made no noise when they moved stealthily throughout the forest. Her chest began to heave, and she gazed around, wondering which way the village led to. It must be back the way she had been running from. Yet, where was that? Her mind had been so oblivious, and just now she had pivoted slowly several times, glancing anxiously about her. Her stomach felt sick as she realized she did not know. *If only John...* The tears welled up in her eyes again, and now she felt she could retch. "Oh, John!" she mumbled. Suddenly something grasped her shoulder.

She screamed.

"Hush!" the words were harsh. "'Tis only I."

She would not have dared turn her head had she not recognized the voice. "Joshua!" she hissed indignantly. "How could you frighten me so?"

He gazed down at her, his hazel eyes flashing. "I should think you would be pleased upon my presence, considering you foolishly walked off and became lost."

"I am *not* lost," she replied fiercely, self-consciously wiping away the tears on her cheeks.

"Is that so?" Joshua said, his voice taunting. He leaned his elbow against a tree, shifting his musket to his other shoulder. "Which way then is Plimoth?"

Hope crossed her arms, frustration welling up inside of her. "Must you be such a nuisance?" she cried bitterly.

Joshua gave a snort of laughter, which in turn gave Hope's numb spirits a sudden work out, for they flared angrily, and her pale cheeks flushed. "Very well," Joshua replied a moment later. "Follow me, if you will."

"Suppose I do not?"

Joshua tossed her a half-grin over his shoulder. "Then you shall be forced to find your way back alone."

Hope squirmed, gripping the folds of her cloak. "I will

Cry of Hope

come with you," she said between gritted teeth a moment later.

"Very good," Joshua replied approvingly. "But first I shall show you something I think you will appreciate knowing." His voice suddenly grew pensive.

Curious, Hope followed him as he cut a path through the thick wood, seeming to know which direction he headed, though Hope was utterly lost. Everywhere she looked beheld the same homely shrubs and bare trees, each trickling with cold melting snow.

Over brush and under branches, they seemed to stride for an hour—though in actuality it was a mere fifteen minutes—when suddenly, before Hope could blink, they were standing in a clearing. Over a few hills she saw the peek of a roof, and she asked in surprise, "Are we near the common house?"

"Yes."

She gazed around, noticing it was a hill that looked as if it had been swept by a flood, for it was rocky and bumpy, rising up in various places and covered with jagged stones. "Why are we here?" she asked cautiously.

Joshua glanced at her sharply. "Be careful where you tread." His hazel eyes pierced into hers, conveying with look rather than words.

Hope started. She glanced around her, finding she stood on a small mound and leapt off, tumbling to the ground. She gasped, trembling. "Joshua!" she cried, tears welling up in her eyes. She clutched her cloak and peered around her, frightened. "Oh!" she cried, "Oh! Where is John?"

"That is why I have brought you here," he said, turning and slowly walking toward a tree near the forest on the right, watching closely where he stepped. Hope stood with shaking knees and imitated his careful movement, shuddering each time she came to a slightly mounded point of land. She dared not wonder who lay beneath that soil and hurried along as fast as she would allow herself.

At length she looked up and saw Joshua kneeling beneath a bare willow tree, nestled at the edge of the wood. It was there she caught sight of a subtle knoll of dirt. She gasped and leapt over the last distance span, collapsing on her knees by John's grave.

"Oh, John, John!" she sobbed, burying her face in her cloak. For a long time she knelt there, weeping. Joshua sat silently nearby, watching her and winking back tears.

"Oh, Joshua!" she gasped at last. "Oh, he fought so hard! He tried to fight the fever! He tried, he tried! But he lost!"

Joshua shifted. "Aye," he whispered, "I have never before known John to lose a battle." Hope gave a shuddering wail, but Joshua continued, "And he did not lose this one."

The abrupt remark brought a sudden lull in Hope's weeping, and she glanced up at him quizzically.

"He won in a different way, child. The fever was a mere testing—an endurance he had to bear before he took the last steps home. I suppose you know after a long, wearisome day, when you are running toward your home, the last few steps can seem the hardest. That is what John was bearing. It was not a battle in the least; it was crossing into the home where he belongs."

The tears did not cease. "His home? His *home?* Where is his home?"

Joshua gazed at her, an unreadable expression in his eyes. At last he leaned back against a tree and lay down his musket. "His home, Hope, is where his Father lives. Perchance he spoke to you of it?"

Hope frowned.

Joshua sighed, "I suppose if he had he had spoken in plainer terms. He has gone to God, Hope. God is his Father. God called to him, just as your father would call to you. When your father calls you, you run to him, do you not?"

"Not always."

A soft laugh escaped Joshua's lips. "You are a rebellious child, Hope Ellison."

"You are a beguiling son, Joshua Mansforth," she shot back, flushing.

"Yes, well..." Joshua glanced away, his grin vanishing. "No longer."

Hope knitted her eyebrows together. "How do you mean?"

Joshua waved his arm across the field before them. "How many mounds did you leap over, Hope? Many, I am sure. Do you suppose most families on the *Mayflower* remained unscathed?"

Hope's mouth dropped. "Did your father—"

"And my mother."

"Why was I not informed?"

"Perhaps you were not listening."

Hope opened her mouth before slowly closing it without remark. Her tears flowed rapidly as she glanced back at John's grave. "Why was he called?"

Joshua would not meet her gaze. He swallowed before saying dully, "I do not know. He took John for a purpose we shall never understand or find out, perhaps."

Hope wiped her nose on her sleeve and gazed at the

mound of dirt before her. She brushed her finger across it, suddenly picturing John's soft brown eyes and long strides, his healthy tanned cheeks and flapping white shirtsleeves. The little cowlick curled on his forehead. His dark hat that would occasionally fly off his head, for Mother had made it a mite too large. "Oh, John," she breathed, longing to give him a last embrace, to confide in him her hopes and fears.

"Come now," Joshua at last broke the incessant gasps, as he sighed and stood. "We must investigate the common house."

She caressed the mound of dirt by the willow tree, bemoaning the return to the common house. But Joshua was insistent, and Hope found herself trudging up the hill after him.

"You ought to at least look at the structure, Hope," he said, a bit of the old playful tone slipping in. "I had a hand in building it."

But Hope looked up at him with blurry green eyes. "Did John take part in the building of it?" she asked hoarsely.

Joshua swallowed. "He did."

"Then I shall treasure it."

And they both hastened up the last hill.

"Hallo, Hope!"

The words were spoken with a familiar buoyancy that must come from only one person. Hope's heart leapt. "John!" she screeched and pivoted, finding herself face-to-face with her late brother. Yet, he seemed no longer her late brother, but alive, standing tall in front of her. He grinned, asking innocently, *"What?"*

"You... you had gone," she whispered, her heart thumping.

"Had I?" he asked, gazing down the beach. Hope hadn't realized she was standing on it. The water lapped mesmerizingly against the shore, and she felt dizzy listening to it.

Suddenly John grabbed her hand and tucked it through his elbow. "Come now," he said with a grin, *"allow me to show you the plantation."*

Hope nodded and began walking up the hill with him. Her mind whirled. Suddenly she wiggled her fingers. She gasped and glanced at her arm. Emptiness met her, and her hand fell to her side with a thump. "John?" she cried out, glancing sharply around her. *"John, where did you go?"*

A shadow passed over her eyes, and she glanced up. The sun had disappeared, leaving a dark cloud hanging low overhead. A fog rolled in swiftly from the sea, blocking all vision, and Hope suddenly screamed, "John, where are you? John? John, come help me!"

There was no answer.

She groped in the dark, trying to find a familiar structure, trying to reach the common house. She strained her blinded eyes to see ahead. A faint flicker of light could be distinguished in the haze. Hope struggled toward it. Suddenly she stumbled, hurtling to the ground and gashing her leg against a sharp stone. "Help!" she screeched. "John! John, where did you go? Why have you left me?" Her heart crumbled. She glanced up, only to see the one light vanish from sight for good.

Hope awakened with a start. She gasped as darkness

threatened to suffocate her. Frantically she groped around, ripping away her coverlet. A flood of yellow light washed over her, and shafts of morning sunshine poured through the open door. She glanced down at her hands, finding the woolen blanket clutched with white fingers. She shuddered, remembering her dream, and her heart felt tight. She tossed the blanket aside, wrapped her cloak around her, and ran out the door.

    A cold breeze whipped her hair back from her face and wailed in her ears, but she kept on until she reached John's grave. There she stopped and sat down, leaning against the maple tree. "Why did you leave me?" she whispered, tears trembling in her eyes. She gazed down at the small mound of dirt, silent. At length she took a shaky breath and said softly, "Do you remember? A long while ago, when sitting in front of our Holland home... you asked how I would manage without you. I had said that I would die." A painful smile stole her countenance for a breath of a second. "I thought I might tell you that I did. My *heart* has died." She wrapped her shaking fingers around her knees as she wept. Tears streamed down her cheeks, dropping like scars on her woolen skirt. The world was hushed around her for a long while, until a voice suddenly said softly, "I thought I might find you here."

    Hope gulped and glanced up. "Hallo," she muttered, wiping her nose.

    Joshua said nothing but sat down a few feet from her, leaning against a pine tree. He laid his musket across his knees, fingering its shape. A bird twittered.

    Finally she mumbled, "My brother. I did not merely lose my brother." Joshua was still, watching her intently. Hope lifted her tear-streaked face, saying in a tremulous voice,

"I have lost my heart."

"Aye," Joshua said softly, "that can leave a hole in your life."

"I do not understand it," Hope suddenly cried out, tears streaming down her cheeks. "My life was comfortable, content, in Holland—then it all began shattering beneath me when we left. Constance, my nearest and dearest friend, was lost to me—Holland, my only home that I love more than any other land was left behind—and now my brother, the only person on earth whom I cherish was wrenched away! Why has it all crumbled beneath me? Why has the world chosen to torment me? Why has the God that we preach incessantly hurled it all at me?" She shook, burying her face in her knees. Joshua was silent for a long while. At last he said, "Some lives need to be broken down in order to be built up."

"But why must it be that way for *me?* Why must everything safe be torn away from *me?*" she pleaded, her voice muffled by her skirt.

"I think you must ask yourself that question, Hope."

She said nothing. At length she lifted her face and whispered in a haggard voice, "All I want is *hope.*"

Joshua gazed at her. "The only place you will find that hope is in the arms of Jesus," he said softly. She rubbed her eyes and gulped. Joshua tilted his head, looking her in the eye. "And He is *begging* you to run to Him."

Hope stared at him a moment. "You truly believe that?" she murmured.

"With all of my heart."

CHAPTER XXI

Dawn

The evening light poured through the open doorway. Most of the congregation had assembled down at the cottage down the hill. It had been completed that day, and excitement had mounted in everyone around. However, Hope hadn't felt as enthusiastic as they, and very soon, after taking a look around the completed structure, she wandered back up the hill and entered the common house. It was peaceful inside, but Hope felt agitated, and a longing she could not explain had pressed upon her heart. Was it a desire for hope? Indeed, it felt like it.

    Why did she not feel as eager as everyone else concerning the cottage? Why was every day ending with the feeling that proverbial threads were left untied, as if the sun had slipped between her fingers and lowered below the horizon before she had a chance to know why the day did not feel complete? Why was her heart still feeling wrenched out of her chest, leaving a black emptiness? She sighed and pressed her hand to her forehead, leaning her elbows on her knees. She did not understand. There was so much she did not understand. Why was life so complex, yet empty at the same time? She swallowed. Joshua's words slipped back into her mind, and she glanced up at the leather Bible lying on the wooden table.

A sudden vivid picture came into her mind. A man—Jesus—hanging on a crude wooden cross, His face smeared with perfect blood. His eyes were riddled with excruciating pain, but He bore it steadily with... love? A wave swept over her, filling her eyes and nostrils with stinging, salty tears. How could He bear it so? *Why* would He bear it so? She suddenly began recalling vast amounts of sin and rejection she had become guilty of—indeed, had it been her entire fourteen years? Her entire fourteen years she had been pushing this... this *love* from her heart?

She choked and stumbled across the room, grasping the thick book in her hands. Shafts of golden sunlight illuminated the pages as she dumped it open on her lap, her eyes falling across the words. "Why art thou cast down, my soul? and why art thou disquieted within me? wait on God: for I will yet give Him thanks: He is my present help and my God."

"Oh, God!" she cried, her hands roughly flipping the pages in agitation. "Oh, God! You took my brother! Why? For what reason could you hurl such a burden upon me? You have left a hole in my heart—and 'tis *empty*. He was the one treasure I loved most. God, why did you take him from me?" Tears rolled down her cheeks, dropping on the Bible. She tried to brush them off, but they left a shining smudge on the page, illuminating several words. "For where your treasure is, there will your heart be also."

Her hand flew involuntarily to her lips, and she stared

at the verse for a long while. She ruffled through more pages, her eyes scanning the words. "Thou shalt therefore love the Lord thy God with all thine heart, and with all thy soul, and with all thy mind, and with all thy strength."

Hope's hands began to shake. "I haven't loved You." It was a whisper that fell from her lips, and an overwhelming awe caused her to pause for a long moment.

At length, she again began flipping pages, scanning verses as she went. "But God setteth out His love toward us, seeing that while we were yet sinners, Christ died for us." *I knew that.* Suddenly she froze. Did she know that? It was a fact forced into her mind since birth, but had she understood the impact?

Suddenly the Bible slipped from her hands, tumbling onto the floor. She bent to grab it, but with a cry of disappointment, she saw that her place was lost. She bit her lip. Suddenly she gasped. Her finger fell involuntarily across the verse that read: "Now faith is the grounds of things hoped for, and the evidence of things that are not seen." She felt tears start to her eyes, and her eyes scanned the words over again.

As long as we have faith, hope can never die. Her brother's words rang throughout her head. "Faith and hope," she whispered in wonderment. "You cannot have one without the other. They are intertwined."

Her heart ached. Yet, how was one to obtain faith? She sighed, leaning her chin on her fist. She absently began turning pages, all the while feeling that she was incapable of understanding such a complex subject.

Her eyes fell upon words—words that at first flew past her head, but suddenly struck her as deserving of attention.

Cry of Hope

She read them again. "This then is the message, which we have heard of Him, and declare unto you, that God is light, and in Him is no darkness. If we say that we have fellowship with Him, and walk in darkness, we lie, and do not truly. But if we walk in the light as He is in the light, we have fellowship one with another, and the blood of Jesus Christ His Son cleanseth us from all sin. If we say that we have no sin, we deceive ourselves, and truth is not in us. If we acknowledge our sins, He is faithful and just, to forgive us our sins, and to cleanse us from all unrighteousness."

She pressed her fingers to her lips, suddenly comprehending for the first time in her life the words of truth that now slipped into her heart from the worn pages. *He* cleanseth us from all sin. *He* is light. *He* is faithful and just.

"Has it truly never been me all along?" she whispered. Suddenly, with a wringing of her heart, the words sunk in. Tears prickled in her eyes, rolling down her cheeks. "The faith does not come from my own efforts, does it God? The faith is Yours, just as the hope is Yours and the forgiveness is Yours. Oh, God, all I really need is You!" Her fingers trembled, and she slipped down on her knees, burying her face in her fists. "'Tis You! God, how could You be willing to suffer Your holiness to give to me the extent of Your mercy? How could You sacrifice all, even Your treasured Son, in order to present me with the fullness of Your hope? How could *I*, the receiver of Your precious gifts, despise and reject You? How could I, God? How could I?" She wept.

Finally, with her lips silent, her heart cried out to the true King, begging for relief from the burden upon her weak shoulders. "I am just a foolish wretch in need of Your forgiveness. I cannot bear this load upon my back. I cannot take the knife of pain wedged in my chest. I need You. I cannot imagine how You should enter the dirty crevices of my heart, how You should desire to make Your home there. But... but I *do* believe You will. Come and be with me, God. Come."

She wept tears. Tears of sorrow that abruptly led to tears of joy. He had come. He was there at that very moment, and He was so strong, so real, so *good* that it hurt. An overwhelming peace enveloped her heart, as the burden of guilt and pain was cast out and replaced with the tender image of Him. Hope smiled. It was a smile of purity that had never once appeared on her face in all the years of her life. She lifted her eyes to the sunset pouring through the open doorway, whispering, "For You are my hope."

Hope awoke early the next morning. It was barely gray out-of-doors, and she knew the sun would be breaking over the horizon soon. She glanced around the common house. Everyone was asleep still. How still and quiet and peaceful it was! Uncannily, the usual snores and snorts had stopped. Many a time Hope had thought ruefully what a noisy congregation they seemed to be. Yet, now everyone was sleeping peacefully.

She gazed out the door, breathing in deeply the warm air of March's end. How fresh the morning smelled to-day! Her feet began pattering down the lane as she took delicious breaths of the gorgeous morning air around her. The dew still stood on the grass, and her feet tingled from the cold drops of water. However, she kept on, heading down the hill toward the beach.

Perchance the morning Jesus rose from the grave smelled just as sweet as this. She stopped as the thought crossed her head. She smiled. *I daresay it smelled even sweeter.*

She gazed about her. The common house stood behind her on top of the hill, the new cottage to her right, and oh! the ocean! It stretched out before her, boasting of miles and miles and miles of lapping water. Streaks of golden light above the horizon had already begun to hint of the forthcoming sun, tinting the gray waters a shiny creamy-gold. *'Tis a lovely day for Easter morn*, she thought with a smile and skipped down to the inviting beach.

The sand warmed her tingling feet, and she sat down on the soft surface, gazing at the stretch of water before. Before she could sit in silent thought long, however, a burst of orange hue shot across the morning sky as a ball of fiery colour peeked above the horizon. Hope's rapturous face was stained a fierce golden, and her mouth dropped at the spectacular display before her. "*How* have I managed to slip by this beauty day after day?" she cried out, standing up and throwing her arms back, as if catching the sun's dancing rays in a rhapsodic embrace. A bird twittered from somewhere behind her, awaking the entire clan, until the whole forest was filled with the happy laughter of chirping.

Hope ran down to the sandy surf, dipping her toes in the freezing water and kicking up a spray, sending glistening water droplets splattering through the air before they softly landed on her hair. "Oh, I do love it!" she cried, her heart so full of light air that it caught in her throat and nearly strangled her.

The long, sharp grass slashed at her ankles as she hurried down the hill behind the common house. Suddenly she stopped short, examining a small white flower growing beneath an old oak tree. Her fingers caressed the delicate petals for a moment before she grasped the stem and tore it from the root with a jerk. She held it close to her chest as she darted the rest of the way down the hill, dropping to her knees by a small mound of dirt.

"Hallo, John," she murmured, choking as tears rose in her throat. She fingered the flower for a moment before gently placing it on the grave. Her eyes suddenly blurred, and she bit her tongue, burying her face in her knees. "I love you so," she sobbed in a muffled voice.

For a long while she sat motionless there, excepting for an occasional heaving of her back. She was unaware of the figure that slipped in behind her, leaning an arm against a tree with glistening eyes.

At last Hope pulled her face up from the folds of the skirt, gazing at the little white flower and saying with a small smile between her tears, "I do wish to tell you something. Jesus took me in His arms for the first time yesterday. I suppose you would have been overjoyed to know it, for... for I realize now you were closer to Him than I had known." She pressed her lips together, her heart feeling stabbed with pain. She gasped, "Oh, it hurts still! But do not worry, brother. He will see me through." She paused, clutching her skirt in her fingers. "I just miss you," she whispered.

A step from behind startled her, and she looked up

to see Joshua sitting down next to her, quickly dashing a tear off his cheek. He swallowed and said nothing, and Hope gazed back at the mound of dirt with the single white blossom nestled on it. "He was a good brother," she said, tears trembling at her eyelashes.

Joshua nodded. He was silent a moment before saying, "I think he deserves more remembrance than a small flower."

Hope wiped her nose and nodded.

Joshua took out a short knife and began slashing at the willow tree behind the grave. After several minutes, he sat back on his heels, and Hope leaned forward to read what he had carved.

John Ellison
A loving brother, true friend,
and child of the Most High.
Anno Domini, 1604 – 1621.

"Oh," Hope breathed, tracing the letters with her finger. "'Tis perfect," she whispered. "'Tis *quite* perfect."

CHAPTER XXII
Restoration

The cool dark daub oozed between Hope's fingers as she pushed it onto the wall, packing it around the wattle. She liked the mushy feel of the earth on her hands. It felt comfortingly familiar to the childish mud pies she and Constance used to make when they were young, and it brought back a bittersweet nostalgia for the old days.

The old days. She cracked a wry smile at the words. Why, her thoughts sounded as if she were years and years old! That would not be for a long while yet.

She gave a hard pat at the wall, then rubbed her fingers together, enjoying the cool feel of the mud. Suddenly she heard voices outside, echoing against the walls of the dark cottage. One was Father's voice, angry and hard. She could not make out what he was saying, but at length he marched off, and Hope peeked out. He was entering the common house, his shoulders rigid. She sighed and wiped her hands.

She glanced back in her bucket, noticing she was out of daub. She'd have to have Joshua mix some more.

Cry of Hope

She picked up the wooden pail and stepped out-of-doors, squinting in the sudden sunlight after the dark shelter. A fresh breeze blew, chilly but refreshing, and she headed down the hill, swinging the bucket in time with her steps.

Joshua was chopping wood at the bottom of the slope, near the trees where the ocean could be glimpsed through the tangle of branches separating the hill from the beach. He looked up as she approached.

"Could you be spared to mix up some daub for me?" Hope asked, setting the bucket down at his feet.

Joshua nodded, wiping his forehead. "Indeed, I could." He glanced around before whispering, "'Twould be a relief to step away from this woodpile. It must all be cut before sundown." He looked at it contemptuously. "But I would be glad for a break. I will have it ready for you in nigh ten minutes. Perhaps your mother has something you could help with while I stir it up?"

Hope scowled. "I suppose she might. Shall I go see?"

"That was rather what I was suggesting." Joshua's eyes twinkled.

Hope crossed her eyes at him and said, "Very well, Commander Mansforth." She saluted, imitating the sailors, and trudged back up the hill.

The ocean breeze whipped her hair in tangles around her face, as if the strands wished to fly out of her mob cap altogether. She glanced around as she neared the top, marveling at how big the ocean was. It was like the fathomless sky, only tangible and *wet*. She giggled to herself and darted the rest of the way up the hill. She started for the door, but hearing sharp voices inside she slowed. She recognized them to belong to Father and Mother, so she slipped next to the doorway and peeked in.

Father was standing, facing the hearth with his back to the door, his heavy shoulders drooping. "Abigail," he said suddenly, his fingers twitching, "was it a mistake?"

Mother sat at the table, her forehead in her hand. "That is not for me to answer," she said at last, her voice clogged. Hope was startled to see her shoulders heave as a tear slid down her thin cheek.

Father turned, sitting heavily in a chair. Rapping his knuckles on the table a moment, he then buried his rough face in his hands in frustration. For a long while he sat motionless, as Mother remained silent, her cheeks pale.

Hope shifted quietly, hiding herself behind the doorway. Eavesdropping was a subconsciously forbidden act, but she could not help the burning curiosity that threatened to overwhelm her. She peeked her head back around, and her heart nearly dropped out of her chest.

Father's back heaved. It was still a moment before it heaved again, and a visible tear rolled down his cheek. "Oh, Abigail," he murmured bitterly. "He was my son."

Hope's throat caught, and her hand flew to her mouth as she tried to hold back an anguished gasp. *John.*

"Please don't!" Mother whimpered, her eyes red as she rubbed her face across her arm, her lips trembling.

Father sat frozen, staring at the table with glazed eyes. He shook his head, his lips parted in disbelief. "He was my son."

Mother sobbed.

"My son, Abigail! My son!" He barked the last words out, slamming his hand on the table as he erupted from his seat. He strode to the wall, leaning his forehead against it.

Grasping the disheveled hair on his forehead, he pulled at it in anguish. "I have lost him," he moaned. "Oh, I have lost him."

Mother rocked back in forth in her chair, mumbling to herself.

"Why has our family suffered since Robert was lost?" Father cried, pacing around the room. "Had I not allowed my brother to join the group of sailors on that foolish little voyage across the Atlantic on a single ship, he would not have become lost. Mother's heart would not have broken." He stood breathing heavily, reliving moments of the past. "I tried. I tried to use better judgment when Father died, Abigail. But I failed."

He began treading the floor, his hands behind his back. "Robert died—and why? Because of a choice I made—*I* made!" He pounded his chest wrathfully. He paused a moment, his hands dropping to his sides. "And John. He was right, Abigail. Oh, he was right!" He covered his face with his hands.

"How do you mean?" Mother whispered, watching him as the tears streamed down her ruddy cheeks.

Father was silent a moment. He gazed into the hearth, his eyes reddening. "He mentioned the winter storms. He said it would not due to waste time," he murmured softly, a sense of astonishment glistening in his eyes. "He said to leave the *Speedwell* behind long before we did. Had we listened to him—had *I* listened to him..." He looked at Mother, tears rolling down his cheeks. "He could be here to-day."

"But 'tisn't your fault!" Mother cried, clasping her hands. "You did not know!"

"Did I?" he asked sharply, staring hotly into the hearth. "Had I shown him the respect he deserved..." He groaned.

"John did deserve respect, Abigail. But I did not give it to him. Abigail," he whispered, his face growing haggard, "I never gave it to him. He never knew I *cared* for him."

"Oh, don't, don't!" Mother wailed, burying her face in the hands.

Father gazed at the hearth. "He was the greatest son I could ever have asked for," he said in disbelief. "And I brushed him away. Why? Why have I always come to the wrong verdict concerning such matters? Why have I always been wrong?" Father was weeping now, visibly weeping. "He never knew I *cared*," he moaned to himself.

"And me?"

Hope stood at the doorway, tears pouring down her cheeks. "I have never known you cared," she accused bitterly. "John never knew you cared. You hurt him, Father. He wanted your respect." Her voice was hard, grudging, as she spit stinging swords at her grieving father. Her heart trembled, bruised from the past childhood that was trampled upon by his gruff feet, having been broken from mistakes during her early years. Her eyes bore into him, blurred from the anguished tears that poured from her heart.

Father gazed at her, tears of agony trembling like ice shards in his beard. All the usual ferocity had gone from his dark eyes; the resentment he carried had crumbled beneath him. He was pleading.

She stood, trembling, her hands behind her back. Taking a step forward, she stared hard at him. "Me?" she asked, her voice shuddering. "Do you love *me,* Father?"

He shook, his lips moving, as he opened his arms. Hope stood still a moment; then, with a fresh flood of tears, she ran into them and clung to him. She felt his arms trembling as he clutched her head to his shoulder, rocking back and forth. "Do you *love* me, Father?" she cried again, burying her face in his shoulder as the grief confined within the walls of her heart for seven years now suddenly burst forth. "*Do you?*"

"Of course, daughter," he whispered at last, setting her in front of him as he collapsed into a chair. He roughly brushed the tears from her face, ignoring the ones running down his own chapped cheeks. "Why do you think we came to this country?"

Hope gazed at him in wonderment, biting her trembling lip. "You took me from my homeland," she said, looking into his face searchingly as the bitterness pierced through her eyes. "You forced me to come to a place I did not wish to come; now you tell me it is for the reason that you love me? Was it not for your own sole purpose?" She shoved the tears that continued to stream down her cheeks.

Father took her face in his trembling hands. "'Twasn't for I, daughter. 'Twas for you—your heart, your mind, and your future. For, whether you would believe such a thing or not, I know things that you do not. I do not wish to see you influenced by pompous ideas in Holland. I wish your future to be free of wars and possible bondage that would by chance appear in that country—'twas for *you*, your children, and their children that we came here."

Hope stared at the floor, tears blurring her vision.

Father took her shoulders, bending to look her in the eyes. "Seeing that now, do you love *me*, daughter?" he repeated her own question in a shaking voice.

She was still a moment. At last she looked up at him, her eyes stinging. "I always have," she whispered.

Mother made a sudden noise and kissed her hair, while Father gazed at her with such gratification and love that she felt she had finally gained an important aspect of her life that had been missing ever before.

CHAPTER XXIII

Samoset

"Dinner is nearly ready," Mother announced as Hope walked into the common house, lugging a wooden pail full of water. She squinted as she stepped indoors, feeling nearly blind after the light of the noonday sun. "What shall we be having?" she inquired eagerly, peering into the iron pot.

Mother glanced at her and said wearily, "Pottage, Hope. Were you expecting anything different?"

Hope groaned rudely and replied, "No; I was *hoping*."

Mother gave her a stern look before pivoting to help Priscilla stack trenchers. "Call the men now, dear, would you?"

Hope nodded and wiped her hands on her apron, bounding to the door. She opened her mouth for the declaration, but suddenly a shrill shriek overtook her words, bringing Mother running to her side. Hope raised a trembling finger, pointing to a tall figure walking swiftly toward them from the woods.

"Oh, dear God," Mother breathed, clutching Hope's

shoulder tightly, "'tis the Indians."

Hope paled and found herself clinging to Mother's skirts like a frightened little child. "Oh, Mother, what shall we do?" she gasped, burying her face in her apron.

"Hush, child," she murmured, giving her shoulder a squeeze. She slipped inside and took down a heavy musket from the wall, taking care to see it was loaded.

"No, Goodwife Ellison!" Priscilla suddenly cried, springing forward and touching Mother's arm. "He does not appear to be armed. We cannot frighten him away before knowing his purpose in coming."

Mother looked at the young woman a moment, before turning silently and placing the musket back in its place. "We shall wait and see his purpose," she murmured quietly. Turning around, she looked at Priscilla, saying bravely, "You and I shall stay here. Hope, dear, you run down and fetch Father and Elder Brewster and the rest of the men. Tell them of this Ind—" She froze and looked stiffly behind Hope, who turned and found herself staring up at a pair of piercing black eyes.

"Greetings, English women," the Indian said calmly.

Hope turned and fled. She rushed down the hill, her heart throbbing. "Father!" she burst out, clutching her trembling hands to her chest, "Father, come quickly!"

He stepped out of a structure, asking sharply, "What is it, daughter?"

Hope gasped and cried out, "Indians, Father. There is an Indian in the common house."

Father said nothing more but grabbed his musket, shouldered it, and strode up the hill. Hope stood trembling a moment before Joshua stepped down from a roof and asked

177

anxiously, "What is wrong, Hope?"

She explained it only partly coherently, but he understood and said, "Come along, we must inform the others."

Soon the entire congregation knew of the arrival, and streams of people began running, striding, or trudging up the hill with anxious faces. Hope and Joshua were last, and Hope could not keep her teeth from chattering. Joshua looked down at her and said softly, "We will be alright."

Hope tightened her arms around herself and replied, "I know, but 'tis frightening. There may be groups of them scattered about, all prepared to come massacre or do something horrid." Her voice trembled.

Joshua touched her shoulder lightly and said, "If so, we shall fight them, if they intend on it. However, thus far we have seen only one, and I think we do not have very much to fear. You say the Indian was unarmed?"

"That is what Priscilla noted. I dared not gaze at him long. If you could have seen his eyes! I felt as if they were burning a hole straight through me, they stared so fiercely." She shuddered again.

Joshua nodded, biting his lip. "Come along," he said at last, taking the last few feet up the hill in one stride. "We shall find out for ourselves."

Hope darted to keep up with him and slipped in close behind, peeking at the Indian. He sat cross-legged in front of the fire, calmly sipping a mug of pottage while the entire congregation looked on in silence. Had Hope not been so frightened, she would have burst into laughter at the comic of the scene.

"Samoset," Elder Brewster began hesitantly, "is your

tribe near?"

The Indian shook his head. "I come on own." He finished the pottage and began to speak. "I with tribe Wampanoag of big chief Massasoit. Massasoit *netop.* He welcome Englishmen."

A general sense of relief passed through the congregation, and tensed muscles relaxed slightly. Hope sighed and glanced at Joshua, who was nodding satisfactorily.

"But, sir," Father asked, with a confused frown, "how have you come to know our language so well?"

Samoset nodded gravely. "I not from here. I from east part. I know Englishmen—they learn me. They come fish where I from." He reached and took a hardtack biscuit from the table, and Hope marveled at how tiny the victual looked in his large hand.

As he ate, a glance from Elder Brewster sent everyone out of the common house excepting him, Father, and a few of the other leaders. Hope caught one last glimpse of the Indian as she turned to go, and he met her gaze with penetrating black eyes. She shivered, quickly pivoting and following Joshua and Mother out-of-doors.

CHAPTER XXIV
Patience is a Virtue

Hope gazed at the crackling fire in the hearth—or so it seemed. She, rather, was watching fearfully the intrusive figure stretched on a blanket before the kindling. It was the Indian, and the thought of him, much less the sight of him, sent her heart to her throat.

For a long while she had attempted to sleep, but her fears had kept her awake. Her fatigue nearly drowned her in weariness, but the comfort of rest itself would not come. Though she had tried through her prayers to convince God of allowing her to sleep, He seemingly refused her request, for nothing aided her in her troubles.

Perhaps her fears had subsided, perhaps not, for she was so groggy she could not comprehend it exactly. However, she understood the fact that an unwelcome figure was sleeping not three yards from her, and she refused to relax. Instead, she swung her legs over the side of her hammock and stepped out of bed. Wrapping her cloak around her, she opened the heavy door of the common house and slipped out into the cool air.

An ocean breeze whipped her tangled hair around her face, and it refreshed her, reviving her mind as she stood blinking in the moonlight. Soon, she remembered why she was standing out-of-doors, and the memory of the Indian inside ignited a series of panic attacks that she fancied were kindled by deceiving noises in the forest.

After standing outside the door to the common house, afraid of reentering its smothering walls and afraid of remaining vulnerable in the out-of-doors, she remembered the completed cottage at the foot of the slope where Goodman Hopkins and his family now resided. After a brief moment of consideration, in which she convinced herself she heard the hiss of an arrow, she wrapped her arms around herself and fled down the hill.

Reaching the cottage in safety, a fact that actually surprised her bleary mind, she stopped outside the door, now faced with the much less daunting prospect of intruding the home of a friend. She reached to push open the door when she suddenly paused, staring with astonishment. It was partially gaped open.

She felt fright again rise in her mind, but before she could allow such anxieties penetrate her nerves, she caught sight of a lonely figure on the beach. Confusion welled up inside of her, for it was quite obviously a young girl clad in a white nightgown. A gentle breeze sent a billow of hair floating on her shoulders, and a sudden sense of amazement welled over Hope as recognition began vaguely settling in her mind.

Spurred by curiosity and wonderment, Hope softly padded through the opening in the woods, emerging onto the pale sand. She, upon approaching the girl without attracting notice, began to feel a mixture of memories and emotion stir up inside of her. As she stood silently behind her for a moment, she caught sight of the tears glinting on the girl's face.

Finally she murmured, "Patience Danford."

A catch sounded in the girl's throat as she turned sharply. She gazed at Hope for a long moment before muttering, "And what brings you here?"

Hope was silent. A whistling breeze tickled her hair, and she said shortly, "I might ask the same of you."

Patience closed her eyes and turned away. The tears still streamed down her cheeks, and for a moment, Hope stood silently, trying to imagine why she was out alone on such a night and why the tears so incessantly streamed from her eyes.

Suddenly she recollected the day she last noticed Patience. It was during her bout of fever, when she awoke to find Patience's ill, grief-stricken face staring blankly at her. Hope shuddered, but a sense of awe came upon her, and before she could stop herself, she blurted out, "Did your parents..." Her voice abruptly trailed off.

Patience whipped around. "And has my life ever been of concern to you?" she seethed, her shoulders shaking.

Hope drew back quickly. "I meant no harm..." she began.

Patience interrupted. "My parents' deaths are not what troubles me at the moment," she said, suddenly gaining a haughty perspective and lifting her chin defiantly. It quivered in the moonlight, however, and as a wave crashed around her ankles, she burst into a fit of tears.

Alarmed, Hope led her to a dry position in the sand, where Patience collapsed onto, coiling her arms around her knees and crying miserably. Hope felt truly distressed over her state. "Shall I fetch Goodwife Hopkins? Are you ill?" she inquired gently, hovering over the girl in concern.

"No!" Patience's words bit the air, and Hope fell silent.

At length, the vocal sobbing led to an inaudible weeping, and Patience pressed her cheek against her knees. Her pale face looked so broken, so anguished that Hope felt tears of empathy prickle in her own eyes. She recognized the hurt.

Suddenly Hope caught a glimpse of something white protruding between Patience's clenched fingertips, and she gently reached out and brushed it. "What is this?" she asked softly.

Patience shrank back, exclaiming, "Can you not once leave me to my own affairs?"

Hope felt taken aback. She nearly sent a stinging word at her, but a prick of conscience caused her to stop abruptly and take a deep breath to gain composure. She looked again at the girl, who was bitterly brushing away the tears on her cheeks.

Finally she whispered softly, "God is crying with you."

Patience froze. Slowly she looked up at Hope, and for the first time, Hope saw the sharp, severe pain that had been buried within the glazed resentment she had built up around her. Her dark eyes seemed to have opened, permitting a window to her battered soul, and Hope ached because of it.

At length Patience whispered, "How should you know? You could never understand a childhood spent in grief."

Hope paled. "Can I not?" she said, her voice rising. "Can I not understand?" She began to tremble as the image of her nine-year-old self flashed before her eyes, weeping on the docks of Holland with a sorrow that was never meant to be endured by a child.

When she shook herself, she found Patience gazing at her, curiosity quivering on the brink of her countenance. Hope took a shaky breath, looking down at the sand. "My life was never that of an ethereal painting. My entire world began to crumble when I was but seven years of age. Shall that suffice?"

It was not a question of vexation, but rather a plead, and to Hope's relief, Patience seemed to recognize it. Her eyes drifted down to her hands, and she slowly, gently, unclosed her fists. Hope wiped away a tear that had escaped her eye and peered at the cloth Patience permitted a glimpse of. "Why, 'tis a mob cap!" she exclaimed.

Patience nodded, fingering it with emotion. "'Tis a child's coif," she murmured. A silence followed, and Hope caught the sound of the ocean waves crashing to shore, licking the sand soothingly. Patience seemed to have heard it as well, for she paused, tilting her head.

"Do you understand the immense power of the water? How it can swallow life in a single instant?" she asked.

Hope choked. "Yes," she whispered. "More than you can suppose."

Patience was silent a moment. Finally she turned to look at Hope with a trembling chin, saying bitterly, "Have you ever wished you could go back and change the past that you so contorted with your own foolishness?"

Hope watched her intently, saying not a word.

Patience closed her eyes as the moon kissed her cheek, a single tear glowing as it dripped from her lashes. Finally she whispered, "I had a sister, Hope." She choked, her back shaking again. "I had a sister."

Hope pressed her hand to her lips, a sudden vague understanding forming within her. But Patience wasn't finished.

"Her name was Elizabeth, and I loved her dearly." A small smile crossed her face for a moment, and she looked down at the coif clutched in her fingertips. Taking a deep breath, she said, "She was four years older than I. She possessed the same ragged red hair, the same peaked face. But her eyes... her eyes were blue like the sky of early morning, a constant porthole to the sunny soul within her slight figure.

"When we were both young, I the age of five and she the age of nine, our chores would often take us out to the countryside just outside of Leiden. There we would fetch clothes in need of washing from an elderly lady, who paid our mother to do the difficult work, for she was feeble and of old age.

"One particular day, the wind was very blusterous, and the clouds hid the sun from view. A storm seemed to be creeping upon us when we bid farewell from the woman at her cottage. Elizabeth and I struggled along the road, each carrying a handle to the basket. However, the wind constantly blew the articles of clothing from the hamper, and more often than not we had to stop so that I could run and fetch the scattered petticoats and aprons from the fields or ditches that we passed. This proved hindering, though not troubling until we reached the walkways near the canals.

"The wind picked up as we began struggling along the footpath, and much to our distress, a particular item that we knew to be of value to the woman flew out of the basket and caught in a spindly tree growing over the canal. Before

Elizabeth could warn me, I had scrambled up that sapling and caught hold of the luxurious petticoat. I looked down at Elizabeth to exult over the retrieving, when a gust of wind sent the tree spinning precariously, and the weak branch I balanced upon creaked in admonition.

"I began to shriek then, and no matter the attempt of spoken consolation from Elizabeth, I refused to calm myself and began to wail louder. I suppose that I might have managed to climb safely down from the tree, but all sense had been replaced by hysteria, and I begged my sister to come fetch me.

"As the tree again swung over the canal and the waters loomed below me, Elizabeth must have become truly frightened at the sight of me clinging to so spindly a branch. 'Grasp a moment longer, Patience,' she cried out as she set the basket on the ground and darted toward the tree. 'I am coming.'

"I squeezed my eyes shut and gripped the branch, the petticoat still clutched in my small hands..."

Suddenly Patience paused. She covered her face with her hands, and a gasp escaped her lips. Hope watched her intently. Finally she continued, her voice muffled. "Another gust of wind came. I heard a sickening crack just below me, and a penetrating scream filled the air. I shrieked Elizabeth's name just as the water in the canal swallowed her, extinguishing her entire being as if she were of no value. She was gone."

Patience was weeping again, her face now clutched in the claw-like snare of her fingers. Before Hope realized what she was doing, she had reached out and enveloped Patience in an embrace, her own tears falling fast from her eyes.

Somehow, unsurprisingly, Patience clung back, burying her face in Hope's shoulder. For a long moment, no sound was heard but that of their blended sobs and the unending crash of the sea upon the shore.

At length Patience gasped, "The pain has never gone away. It continues to return, after all of these years, with the same plunge of agony as before. The ache that remains with me day and night almost never ceases. Why is it so? Why can I not ease the pain?"

"Because you truly cannot," Hope whispered back, sitting back and rubbing the tears from her own wet cheeks. "Nor can time ever heal an ache that opened so bitter a wound."

"Why?" Patience cried out, a spasm of tremors running through her.

Hope was silent a moment. "Because," she said slowly, "because one needs a Healer to bind up the wounds." She sat deep in contemplation a moment before saying, "There is a verse in book of Psalms that echoes that thought. I happened to stumble across it the other day. It states: 'He healeth those that are broken in heart, and bindeth up their sores.' Had it not applied to me as well, I should not have taken care to remember it." She fell silent, tracing her finger through the sand as her own pain welled up in her heart again.

Suddenly a hand touched her shoulder, and she looked up to see Patience gazing at her with blurry eyes. Trembling, they suddenly reached out and clung to one another. As the moon slipped behind a wispy cloud, the ocean's incessant call was echoed by the mutual mourning of hearts pierced with the loss of those that could never be retrieved again. Yet, in a way in which Hope was unable to explain, a certain Peace had pacified the raw wound, and she earnestly hoped from the depths of her heart that Patience would experience the same serenity.

The next morning, as Hope emerged from the woods with a pail full from the spring, she nearly ran headlong into Patience. "Oh," she stammered, "hallo."

Patience merely gazed at her. The golden rays of sunlight glistened in the tears that seemed to overwhelm her dark eyes. As Hope reached out to squeeze her shoulders, she returned the embrace fiercely, saying nothing to break the knowing silence that enveloped them with the gentle warmth of peace.

CHAPTER XXV

Bonding

The fourth of April, Anno Domini 1621
Plimoth Plantation

Dearest Constance,
    It is with utter grief that I write to you...
    Hope bit her lip, gazing at the page. She sighed, rolling over on her feathertick. She was in the loft of her family's new cottage; they had settled in that afternoon. Subsequently, Father had declared to them that the *Mayflower* would depart for England the next day, and Mother bid her to write to her friend, if she so wished.
    Hope knitted her eyebrows together as she gazed up at the thatched roof. Constance was now fourteen years of age. An awe suddenly fell over her as she realized how long it had been since she had last seen her friend. Under normal circumstances, they would merely run down to the others' house to state whatever news they had to bear. Now it would

be weeks before Constance received her missive, if it ever reached her.

She turned back to her letter.

It is with utter grief that I write to you. John has died.

"No!" The words involuntarily fell from Hope's lips, and she crumpled up the precious paper and flung it into the farthest corner of the loft. The unfeeling words could never express her pain.

Hope sighed. She missed her friend's companionship.

Suddenly a rap on the ladder caught her attention, and she peeked over the side, finding Patience's slim face looking up at her uncertainly.

"Hallo!" Hope said with a brief smile. "Come up and visit awhile."

Patience scrambled up the ladder, gazing about the room with solemn eyes. "'Tis very nice," she said at last, in such a sober manner that Hope cracked a smile.

Patience leaned against the wall and stared at Hope, her dark eyes unreadable in expression. After a moment, she asked, with soft curiosity, "Do you miss Holland?"

Hope gulped as the subject scraped her heart with the pain of homesickness. "Do you?" she asked at last.

Patience looked uncomfortable, and a flash of pain crossed her face. "I think I shall always associate the place with pain. I daresay I could never form a loving attachment to it."

Hope nodded slowly. Changing the subject, she asked softly, "What were you doing the other night on the beach?"

Patience looked down. "I went down to the sea," she whispered. "I looked over the ocean and thought of Elizabeth. She died in the water. She still sleeps under the murky depths,

I suppose. Ever since then, I slip away occasionally when I miss her. I think of her, and somehow, she does not seem so far away."

Hope nodded, choking. "I know," she said hoarsely. Her eyes drifted back to her discarded paper in the corner, and an idea suddenly struck her mind. Before she could blurt out any of her thoughts, however, the silence was broken by Mother calling Hope to come help fetch supper.

"I had best be going anyhow," Patience murmured, starting toward the ladder.

Hope followed her down, and after thinking fast, asked loudly, "Patience, this house can hold more. Might you come stay with us instead of Goodman Hopkins' family?"

A clatter from the hearth evinced Mother's surprise, and Patience stared at Hope with her expressionless dark eyes. "Perchance," she murmured, and Mother said, to Hope's great relief, "That would be lovely, I must say. Goodman Ellison was saying we need to invite a few from the congregation to stay with us. I shall speak to Goodwife Hopkins to-morrow." She nodded her head firmly, as if to settle the matter, and turned back to the hearth.

Hope met Patience's eyes, and she gave a slight smile and short nod, before slipping out the door. *I do hope I made the right choice,* Hope thought to herself with a sigh, before turning to lay the trenchers on the table.

"Did you finish your letter to Constance?" Mother asked, as she stirred the pottage in the kettle.

Hope paused. "No," she said thoughtfully. After a moment, however, her face cleared, and she said firmly, "But I shall."

"How many are there?" Patience clutched Hope's hand, her pale face looking frightened.

Hope squeezed her arm, trying to keep her voice from shaking as she said, "There cannot be all too many. Besides, I am sure we outnumber them in weaponry. They have those queer branches with string—Joshua said they are bow and arrows, I believe; we have rifles and swords. I am sure we are quite safe."

Even as she said the words, however, she could not help feeling uncertain. The group of Indians emerging from the woods strode purposefully toward the common house—how many there were Hope could not tell, but it seemed the man in the midst of the others stood out in some way, as if a sort of honor had been bestowed upon him by the rest of the men in his tribe. A queer feathered headdress adorned his weathered head, drawing attention to himself by the brightly coloured feathers that brought upon a wild atmosphere surrounding the old man. Indeed, he must have been very old, Hope reasoned, for a mass of wrinkles seemed to ripple across his brown face, accentuating the large nose awkwardly placed a little lower than the center of his head. His face was, actually, so disproportionate it was nearly grotesque.

Standing at the foot of the hill, Hope and Patience had gathered, both feeling much safer being as far from the Indians as possible.

"How long shall they be here, do you suppose?" Patience whispered anxiously.

"Not long, I hope!" Hope replied, squeezing Patience's arm again. "Let us go down to the ocean to wait. It frightens me seeing them here."

Patience agreed, so they strode off quickly toward the sea, darting around the long strip of trees that hid most of the beach from view. Hope rushed to the water, picking up her skirts and dipping her feet in the cold waves. A shriek rose in her throat, and she clapped a hand over her mouth, subsequently dropping her skirt in the water. It was promptly washed over by a foaming wave. "Dear me," she gasped, again gathering up her skirts in her arms, which were by now thoroughly soaked.

"Hope Ellison!" Patience cried. Suddenly she burst into laughter. Startled, Hope forgot her predicament and turned to stare at her. Patience had nearly doubled up giggling. How on earth?—Hope had never seen Patience Danford laugh in all of her life. Nevertheless, her giggles were contagious, and a grin burst across Hope's face. "Come along," she said, beginning to run down the ocean surf, as a wave crashed around her ankles. "Let us race."

Patience, still giggling, kicked up a spray of ocean water and ran after Hope. Down the long stretch of beach they ran, each finding comfort for their fears in the common sport. Back and forth, back and forth they darted gleefully, until Hope nearly bumped straight into Joshua, who had stepped abruptly out of the trees. She skidded to a stop just in time, causing Patience to tumble into her from behind, sending both girls into a heap on the ground. "Oh, dear me!" Patience giggled, while Hope fell into a fit of laughter.

"What foolish children!" Joshua clucked with twinkling eyes, somehow looking as if he did not think them so foolish as he said.

"What news, messenger?" Hope asked, after she had

stood up and brushed her skirts off.

"Oh, we have merely settled a peace treaty with the Indians. That is all," Joshua said with an impish grin, leaning against a tree trunk with the air of someone who knew all.

"How perfectly splendid!" Hope clasped her hands together delightedly, while Patience pranced in place to show her relief.

"I thought you would be pleased," Joshua chuckled.

That evening, Hope started out for the spring, swinging the bucket casually, feeling comfortable knowing the fact that the Indians would not harm them. She padded through the woods, her bare feet licking the soft pine floor as she made her way to the cool spring. As she dipped the pail in gently, she suddenly caught sight of a brown face peering in the reflection. She squealed and jumped back, dropping the bucket into the spring.

"Careful, *nicksquaw*," the Indian said, swiftly catching the pail before it sank to the bottom, setting it on the forest floor. Extending a hand in the English way, he said clearly, "I am Squanto. I am friend of the Englishmen."

Hope stared at him incredulously, at last timidly taking his large hand with her small one. "I... I am Hope Ellison," she said uncomfortably, wondering if it was the proper way to greet an Indian.

"Ah, Hope Ellison," he nodded wisely, "I know *noeshow*." He leaned forward, saying kindly, "That is Wampanoag for a father."

"Oh," Hope nodded. She wrinkled her forehead.

"How is it you know the English language?"

"I have lived in England," was the unexpected answer.

Hope could not hide her shock. "How so?" she asked, forgetting all manners in her curiosity.

He smiled. "It be a long story. Perchance I tell you someday."

Hope nodded, almost smiling herself. "How long are you staying?" she asked, trying to hide her anxiety.

"I hope to stay always," he replied, giving Hope another start. He smiled again at her reaction, saying, "This was my peoples' land, you see? They all dead. But I like to live where my people lived."

"Oh," Hope said again, rather stupidly.

Squanto looked up at the treetops. "Light fading. Must be getting home, Hope Ellison." He picked up her water bucket, dipping it in the water and drawing up a pailful. "I carry this home and see you get there safely."

So Hope followed him as he lightly led the way home through the woods, looking as if he were part of nature himself by the graceful way he moved through the trees and brush.

Upon reaching the threshold, he set it down by the doorway. "Farewell," he said, nodding solemnly and striding up the hill toward the common house, where the braves of the Wampanoag tribe were staying.

"Farewell," Hope replied faintly, watching him. She turned slowly around, before stopping abruptly, for three pairs of eyes were watching her incredulously.

"Did frightened Hope just speak to an Indian?" Father asked, as a new look of teasing twinkled in his ordinarily stern eyes.

"I think she felt brave for once," Mother said, smiling,

as she stirred the pottage in the wooden bowl on the table.

"Oh, come now, she *had* to talk to him, for I am sure he spoke first!" Patience declared, looking at Hope with shining eyes.

Hope gazed about the faces of her family and suddenly burst into hysterical laughter.

CHAPTER XXVI

Homemaking

"Hope, come here, dear."

Giving one final pat to her feather tick in the loft where she had been tidying it after a night's sleep, Hope scrambled down the ladder, landing with a thump on the floor. "Yes, Mother?" she asked, her hair mussed.

Mother stood straight, holding the broom in her hand. She gazed at Hope for a moment, and Hope looked back, wondering what the queer overview was for.

"Yes, Mother?" she asked again, wiping a strand of hair from her cheek.

Mother sighed. "You are a child no longer, Hope Ellison."

Hope squirmed, feeling she could not accurately judge that for herself. It was true, since John's death her aspect on life had changed considerably, but somehow she felt as if she still had every ounce of childish spirit within her.

"Child, you are no longer a child," Mother said, reiterating her statement with a sad little smile. She tapped

Hope's chin with her finger and said, "Dear, it is high time I teach you the notable tasks of homemaking. This spring is not a season too soon. I daresay it will not be long before you have your own home to keep."

Hope's eyes widened. She had assumed she would have her own home to care for one day, of course, and even imagined it, but somehow she had never considered it likely to be so soon. "I am but fourteen, Mother," she reasoned aloud.

"Indeed, but come August you will be fifteen, and Hope, dear, you know I was married shortly after becoming sixteen years of age," Mother replied, turning to sweep the hearth.

Hope felt a jolt in her stomach. "I hadn't considered marrying so young, Mother," she replied sharply, glancing out the door.

Mother smiled a little knowing smile, gazing down at the floor as she swept. "You may wish it sooner than you think, I would venture to say."

Hope crossed her arms, feeling rather frightened by Mother's prediction. *I will not*, she thought, biting her lip.

Suddenly Mother placed the broom on the hook. "Come now." She led the way out the door.

Hope hurried after her. "Where might we be going, Mother?"

"There is no better place to begin homemaking than the garden, Hope. You shall be solely responsible for the vegetation this year; I will tend to the herbs."

"I *alone* am to grow the entirety of our food for the winter?" Hope gasped, her stomach jolting.

"More or less, yes, dear," Mother replied calmly, stopping behind the cottage. She turned to look at her daughter, a smile on her lips.

"Do you truly believe me capable for such a task?" Hope asked in disbelief, furrowing her brow as she gazed across the trampled land.

"No," Mother replied. "However, with my instruction, I daresay you shall manage just fine."

"But what should cause you to bestow such a burden on me?"

"Well, not only must you learn and grow in your capabilities as a homemaker, but very soon there is to be a delicate life brought forth into our family."

Hope blinked. "A new life?" Her heart began to pound.

"Indeed. There is a child within me, Hope, and I daren't strain myself with difficult tasks. You must help me, dear. I haven't a greater need of your assistance than now." Mother paused and watched Hope's face, which had flushed with emotion. "Do you enjoy the thought of this little one?" she asked presently.

Hope was surprised by the earnest concern in which she spoke. Truthfully, she hadn't the faintest clear thought at the moment, for it came as such a surprise it had barely gained consciousness in her mind. Finally, she began to grin. "A new child?" she asked incredulously.

Mother laughed and nodded.

She clapped her hands together. "I wonder, shall it be a boy or a girl? Oh! What will John—" She cut off abruptly, a pang stabbing her heart. With a glance up at Mother, she caught the pain etched across her face. Hope managed a brief smile through the sudden tears that welled up in her eyes. "He would have thought it most wonderful."

Mother nodded, her face pinched.

Turning, Hope caught up a hoe leaning against the side of the cottage. Quickly falling to work, she fought back the pain within her, breathing deeply as she finally let it slip into the hands of the Healer. Eventually, the piercing pain was replaced with a gentle ache. Closing her eyes, she thought fiercely, *John cared for me. 'Tis my duty to care for this little one.* She gripped the hoe in her hands, recklessly hacking at the grassy ground. *And I shall... starting at this very moment.*

As the weeks trotted by Hope spent countless hours working in the little garden. With Mother's surveillance and instruction, and the occasional assistance of Patience, Hope was amazed to see it begin to take shape. The first green shoots to appear delighted her more than she had expected. In fact, she so loathed the idea of destruction to her plants that she implored Father to build her a fence before even Mother considered it necessary. Father, greatly amused by her anxiety, soon appeased her worried mind by constructing her a fence.

The supply of food for the pilgrims increased everyday, for Squanto taught them the knowledge they lacked in finding and cultivating food in the wild land. The sea provided mussels and fish, the forest was bountiful with beasts and wild fowl, and the earth nurtured the plants with the help of Indian proficiency.

During the passing days, Hope found herself growing more and more confident in her abilities of homemaking. With Mother able to do less in the coming weeks, she felt that even she could manage the prospect of her growing weight of chores. And though she did not particularly enjoy the idea, she had already begun to discover the joys of simple satisfaction that came with the completion of an effortful womanly task.

Cry of Hope

CHAPTER XXVII

Summer Days

Spring passed, and summer came. Hope practically lived in her garden, finding an unexplainable comfort among the leafy greenery, taking pleasure in tending the plants as if they were her children. Mother's herbs flourished in the rich soil. The corn in the fields grew tall. Hope, though finding pleasure in all of her vegetables, was particularly fond of her squash, for the orange gourds were both pretty to see and useful to eat—when they were ripe. Hope discovered, in a rather bitter way, that vegetables were better left alone until they were grown to eating size.

She was examining her lettuce one day, touching the delicate leaves, when she became overwhelmed with a desire to taste fresh greens once again. Perhaps they were ready to be eaten, she considered. She peeled back a crisp leaf gingerly. Popping it in her mouth, she promptly gagged.

Suddenly she heard a chuckle behind her. She turned, finding Joshua watching her from the gate with an amused grin on his face.

She glared at him. "How do you do, sir?" she said sharply, with a proper nod that was rather short in giving, for the giver was flustered just at the moment.

His eyes softened as he nodded back, with a sweep of his wide-brimmed hat. "Very well. I came to offer my services to your father. This fence is in dire need of repair, I see. Did an animal break in last night?"

"Yes," Hope said, her eyes sweeping sadly over her lovely turnips that had been crumpled and damaged when she had come to hoe the weeds that morning. "It was a foolish boar that broke in. Father wished for the meat, but the creature was long gone by the time we discovered him having been here."

Joshua nodded, surveying the broken fence. "Well, I will try and strengthen the fence when I fix it—that should keep any creature out."

"Thank you, sir. I should go help Mother in the kitchen—knowing her, she will try and do more than is good for her," Hope said with a hint of amusement, as she opened the gate.

"Very well." Joshua leaned on the fence with a smile. "You are not the same Hope Ellison that ran off on her parents that fateful day in Holland. Do you recall how your brother was working in the mill, unable to keep you compliant? 'Tis a blessing I heard of the news and found you. You were weeping your heart out on the docks of Holland." He gazed at her, a look of understanding in his eyes.

Hope's smile faded. "I recall." She was silent for a moment, before shaking herself and saying, "You *would* be the one to remind me of my childhood follies."

Joshua laughed. A grin teased Hope's lips, and she

brushed past him, heading around to the front of the cottage.

"Oh, and Hope."

She turned.

"I do not recommend tasting more greens soon," he said, with boyish mischief written across his face.

"Not to fear—I would not think of it," she returned with a grimace, before disappearing around the corner of the house.

"Hallo, Mother," she said, finding her mother standing by the doorway idly, with a broom in her hand. A sad look seemed to have come across her face, and Hope took her by the hand, leading her into the house. "Come now, you ought to rest," she scolded teasingly, whisking the broom from Mother's hand and briskly sweeping the floor with it.

Mother smiled at her—an amused smile—saying, "Do not overwork yourself, dear."

"Nonsense! 'Tis *you* who ought not overwork yourself," Hope returned, pausing to stir the pottage in the kettle. "Where is Patience?" she asked, as Mother settled in a chair to study the large leather Bible sitting open on the table. She stroked the worn pages a moment before replying, "She is fetching the water for supper."

"Ah. Oh, dear, are the mussels done?" Hope grasped a cloth and lifted the lid of the pot. "Indeed! Oh, the shells did open nicely this time."

Soon supper was set on the table, consisting of pottage, mussels, and corn cakes with water to drink. Father came in a moment later, followed by Joshua.

"This young man was fixing my fence," Father announced good-naturedly. "I thought it only right to invite him for supper. Have you spread enough for the whole of us, wife?"

"Hope prepared it," Mother smiled.

"But Patience helped," said Hope quickly, flushing under Father's approving look and Joshua's surprised stare.

"I steamed the mussels, and there were plenty tossed in, sir," Patience told him. Hope smiled, for, knowing Patience, the mussels *were* most likely "tossed in," as she honestly and recklessly described it.

"There are plenty of corn cakes, and we shall make do with the pottage," Hope declared firmly, as Father and Joshua pulled up stools, and they all gathered around the table. Taking hold of one another's hands, they bowed their heads as Father said the blessing in his soothing deep voice. "Our Father who art in heaven; we thank Thee for Thy bountiful blessings Thou hath bestowed upon us—food to fulfill our fleshly needs, fellow brethren and sisters in Thy heavenly family to share all joys and sorrows, and Thy peace that settles over mine household. We remain humble in Thy holy presence. Amen."

"Amen," Mother murmured, and Hope echoed it with a resounding thought that seemed to be ringing in everyone's heads. *Amen.*

Hope gently touched the corn's tassel. The late summer stickiness had settled in, warming everything with the sweet smell that indicated the end of the season.

"Harvest shall be soon."

Hope turned, finding Joshua behind her, nodding with his usual calm expression of face. She smiled. "I can hardly wait to taste the delicious squash from my garden."

"Just do not be trying any without Squanto's word of approval. If you keep it up, your face just might stick with that bitter expression, and everyone would fear your approach."

Hope laughed. Ever since that sad day of tasting a green too early, Hope had tasted bits of each of her vegetables every now and again, unable to resist the delicious temptation, and Joshua knew it.

Shouldering her hoe awkwardly, she said, "Well, the sun being low, I think it best to head back home and help Mother with supper. Have you seen Patience to-day? The poor dear scuttles to and fro with her work lately, as if there were a wild boar chasing her. I hardly find a chance to speak to her."

"Home?" Joshua said with a slight smile, taking the hoe from her small hands, as he entirely ignored her last question.

Hope glanced at him with a wince, walking fast down a well-worn pathway. "Perhaps..." she shrugged, looking uncomfortable. Suddenly she stopped, for they had come to the top of a hill. The golden grass of the rolling slopes ahead glistened in the late afternoon sunlight, waving in the occasional breeze until the hummocks suddenly washed into the plantation on their right and the wide, wide ocean ahead. The waters were calm, gently waving with their continuous motion and sparkling with the golden reflection the sun had painted on its surface.

"'Tis beautiful," Hope murmured, drinking it in with a look of wistful satisfaction. "Such beauty always fills me with a sort of awe and longing. A longing for what, I cannot tell, but it is there. I want to be *in* that beauty. I want to feel it wrap me up in a soft embrace. I want to be a part of this glorious land."

"Are you saying that you wish to accept it as your home?"

The words caught Hope off guard, and she glanced at Joshua. He was gazing at her, a soft smile playing upon his lips.

"No." She shook her head sharply. "My home is with the windmills, the tulips, and the canals. Not... not this subtle beauty." Her words ended with an audible sigh that seemed to contradict the uncertain words. Her heart seemed to be tugged to the cool soil beneath her feet, the blue sky overhead, the waving, golden grasses, and the wide ocean itself. But no... Holland was where she should belong.

She looked down at her dusty shoes, feeling uncomfortable. Fortunately, Joshua ended the subject abruptly, for he said, speaking rather fast, "Is that Patience in your garden?"

Hope shielded her eyes from the bright sun, squinting. "Indeed, I believe it is. She had better not be tasting any of my vegetables!" She laughed, following Joshua as he led the way down the hill.

"Speak for yourself," he called back with a chuckle. "You have done it many times already."

"Oh, but that is an act reserved for me, and me only," she returned laughingly and trotted after him toward her cottage.

Patience met them at the gate, leaning on it with a bright smile flashing on her pale face. Her red hair seemed fiery in the afternoon sunlight as she said with twinkling eyes, "Hope, your mother said that you deserve an afternoon of rest, and that you might wander down to the beach if you so wish."

"Oh." Hope was surprised, but she declined, saying, "I had better not. She ought not work herself out so with a child on the way. I shall stay and make supper. I really do not mind it so much."

Patience looked at her, catching her wrist. "I shall stay and help your mother. You need a pleasant rest, dear."

"Oh, but..." Hope said, confused, but finally turned to Joshua, saying, "Perhaps you wish to come with me? I do not prefer to be alone much."

"Ah, that sounds enjoyable, but no," Joshua replied, shaking his sandy head. "I ought to head back to Goodman Hopkins' home and fetch Goodwife Hopkins her firewood. I find living with them to be quite gratifying at most times, for she can prepare the most scrumptious meals." He grinned.

"Oh. Well, farewell then. I shall head down to the beach." Hope forced a smile and slipped down the road, darting down the dusty street toward the inviting water that lay below.

She reached the sand behind the row of pine trees. Bending down, she scooped a handful of the fine mixture, cupping it in her hands as it slipped between her fingertips back to its home below. Suddenly struck with an impulse, she hurriedly unbuckled her shoes, pulling the heavy things off her feet and casting them off near the trees. After she had tugged off her stockings and laid them by her shoes, she pranced around the beach with a girlish smile on her lips, twirling around and around as the late afternoon sun gave way to a brilliant sunset that Hope could see by tilting up her head as she spun. A mixture of gold and fire, turquoise and pink all swirled together in a dazzling collage as she twirled her heart out, dancing on the fine sand.

When she had grown dizzy enough to feel tired, she walked to the water's edge and decided to follow the surf as far as her eyes could see. The waves crashed around her ankles as she strolled on, but after being so hot all afternoon, the cold water felt pleasant, as did the cool breezes and dusky twilight that settled in.

At length she reached a barricade of rocks, upon which breakers crashed with fury, sending foaming mist into the air that delighted Hope. She climbed atop one of the boulders, stepping from rock to rock until she had made her way to a smooth stone away from shore, where she could dangle her feet pleasantly in the water and simultaneously get sprayed from the mist of the breakers ahead.

After staring long and hard to see if she could see the bottom of the dark ocean, she looked up and almost gasped aloud. A single bright star appeared on the horizon, shining bright with its heavenly goodness. John's words suddenly came back to her heart. *"The stars penetrate through the dark sky, glistening and enlightening the soul that will find them... that is where we see the hints of the marvelous things that are to come."*

"Oh, John," she murmured, gazing out over the dark waters and staring with shining eyes at the bright beauty glistening in the sky above. She sighed, whispering, "God, You see it. You *saw* it. You knew that I would emerge from the sorrows of John's death with a renewed sense of You."

She peered at the horizon, almost curiously, saying, "Did You send me here from Holland for that very reason?" She paused a moment. "Now that I have found You, might You send me back? Somehow?" Her heart felt tugged again, and she stroked the rock's rough texture, tickling the water with the tips of her toes. *I wish. I wish.*

"Hope Ellison?"

She jumped, startled, and turned to see the faint outline of a man making his way toward her. She was quite frightened at first, but then squinted, realizing it was only Squanto. She wrapped her arms around her knees, gazing at the single bright star as he sat down cross-legged next to her.

"Hallo," she said softly at last.

Squanto grunted, saying nothing. The silent beauty of the twilight seemed to have enfolded him, too, with its peaceful atmosphere. One by one, many more stars appeared, shining their bright faces upon the two wanderers below, who had made their way into the outdoor splendor with, perhaps, the same sense of tugging on their hearts.

At length, Hope broke the unending silence with a gentle voice. "You once said that you lived in England. How so?"

Squanto sighed, looking steadily up at the night sky. "Englishmen capture me when I a small boy. They make me slave to people of Spain."

"That is horrid," Hope said, watching him attentively.

"Yes, horrid. I was made slave in Spain. But I manage to escape. I got to England, where I live with kind man for many summers. But I miss home. After many more summers, I come back with men—explorers. Now I here to stay. I never leave again." Squanto stared fiercely at the ocean breakers, and Hope knew he meant it with all of his heart.

"I miss my homeland," she said pensively, fingering the folds of her skirt as she gazed at the horizon.

Squanto nodded. "It hurt. I love this land very much."

"I love Holland very much," she whispered. She brushed her cheek, as if wiping away a tear that was not there. She shifted, feeling again the weight of the rough rock beneath her. *I love this land very much.* Squanto's words seemed to ring in her head.

"Why do you love this land so much?" Hope asked, absently stroking the textured feel of the boulder.

Squanto's eyes grew soft. "This land *free*."

Hope stared at him. Her heart trembled as her eyes filled involuntarily.

They sat in silence a while longer, drinking in the sweet night air that settled in around them, until Squanto stood, saying, "We go. It late. I promise mother I fetch you."

"Oh, did you?" Hope asked in surprise. "She must want me. I do hope we haven't been too long. You came quite some time ago."

"No fear. She said to take time." Squanto stepped from rock to rock with agility, turning once to call, "Come, *nicksquaw*. We must not make mother worry."

"You said that you were bid to take your time!" Hope laughed back, jumping from boulder to boulder and desperately praying she would not slip and tumble into the ocean below.

"She said that much time ago. Now we hurry," Squanto called back, beckoning her to come.

So she trotted after him, down the long beach, as she tried to keep up with his quick, long strides. Upon reaching the row of pines, Hope hurriedly slipped on her stockings over her sandy feet and stomped her feet into her shoes.

They walked up the hill, and Squanto slowed his steps to a quiet stroll. A golden light suddenly poured out of an open doorway ahead, and Hope recognized it to be her cottage.

"I do hope I am not late for supper," she said in alarm, partly to Squanto and partly to herself.

A figure stepped outside, peering down the street.

"Why, 'tis Joshua!" Hope cried eagerly, her steps quickening.

She reached the flood of light, and Joshua grinned at her. "How was the beach?"

"Splendid! Twilight is such a beautiful time by the water," Hope said rapturously. "Yet, why are you here?"

"Oh..." Joshua said vaguely, leaning his arm on the doorway. "I believe it has something in mind with the date being August the ninth."

"August the ninth?" Hope's eyebrows knitted together. "But that is the day I was born."

No sooner had the words left her mouth than Patience pounced on her, giving her a fierce hug as she cried out, "Huzzah, dear Hope!" Mother and Father circled 'round her after Patience's warm words, and they gave her a mutual embrace, as Mother said softly, "My dear girl, you are fifteen years of age to-day."

Hope was astonished. "You all remembered?" she asked with a quiver to her voice.

"Of course we did!—well, *they* did and told me. It was all your mother's thought," Patience gushed. "I sewed you a new apron between chores, and we have made your favorite dinner to be eaten with all of us."

"But... but *why?*" Hope felt a tear slide down her cheek.

"Why, because we love you!" Patience said in surprise, as if Hope had just asked the most foolish question in the world.

"I... I love you, too," Hope managed, giving Patience another embrace and burying her tearful face in the girl's tumbled red curls.

"*Noe wammaw ause.*"

It was Squanto, who stood nearby, rather forgotten in the flutter of the moment. "That 'I love you' in Wampanoag," he smiled.

"*Noe wammaw ause*," Hope whispered wonderingly, trying the new words with her own tongue. "*Noe wammaw ause*, Mother, Father. And Patience." She smiled at the red haired girl, who smiled back. Suddenly her eyes caught sight of Joshua, who watched her, his hazel eyes soft in the golden light. Her mouth caught in her throat for a moment, but Patience shook her suddenly, saying, "Come, now, we must have the dinner. I prepared half of it." She gave a delighted laugh as she led the way indoors, and Hope grinned, following her to the bright table inside. "I do believe I am famished," she laughed, sitting down in her place of honor at the head of the table.

CHAPTER XXVIII
Thanksgiving

Harvest had come. Hope was rather overwhelmed by the abundance of her vegetable garden. It was nearly bursting with colourful foods. First, the turnips were pulled, and Hope and Patience spent several long, delightful days gathering as many turnips as they could find. Giggles and sporadic exclamations or jests were heard from the gates many times a day, bringing a boyish smile to the face of a certain young man each time he strode past.

Next, the squash was harvested. Bright yellow, creamy orange, and dark green squashes were carefully tugged from the vines and placed in one of the two girls' baskets before the sun went down.

Then came the corn. What fun they had picking corn! Joshua was bid to join them, along with many of the other children and young people, including determined Constanta Hopkins and impish Francis Billington. Between Joshua's hearty amusement, Hope's spunk, Francis' mischief, Constanta's resoluteness, and Patience's giggles, the days passed pleasantly, full of laughter, sporadic games of All Hid between the tall stalks of corn, and merry jests passed along in the most lively way. Occasionally Squanto would join them, and with him came all the bits of wisdom and pieces of Wampanoag language he threw in, until even the youngest of the children were heard calling their fathers "*noeshow*" and their mothers "*nitka*" before they were bid to use their proper English language that was still a part of their heritage.

The leaves on the trees were now transformed into vivid reds, fierce oranges, and crackling yellows, brightening the forests into a plethora of colours that delighted Hope's beauty-loving eyes. The air was sweet with the smell of late summer hay, shimmering with a hint of crispness mixed in, warning of the approaching winter that was coming faster than anyone could guess. Indeed, no one felt an ease of mind until the last of the harvest was in, the last of the cottages were chinked to ward of winter cold, and the last of the firewood was properly stowed away in shelters. The day everything finally managed to be complete was a relief to all.

That evening, Hope and Patience scurried about between hearth and table, preparing dinner while Mother rested.

"Corn! I dearly love corn," Patience said with a womanly briskness that amused Hope greatly, as she plopped the ears one by one into the kettle

"I prefer the squashes best," Hope replied with a smile, as she tossed together lettuce, onions, and carrots in a bowl. It was a simple delicacy that Mother suggested several months ago, as it provided an extra serving to the meal.

Patience nodded, standing back from the fire and wiping her hands on her apron. "Yes, but I simply love the golden taste when biting into a corn cob."

"*Golden* taste?" Hope asked with a laugh, looking at her friend in the dancing light.

Patience nodded pensively. "It tastes so very golden as the kernels burst in your mouth, does it not?"

Hope laughed, setting out trenchers. "I suppose so, when one looks at it that way."

"Have I some news for you!" Father exclaimed in his deep voice, as he stepped into the cottage from the open doorway. A gust of cool air followed him as an autumn breeze drifted in, ruffling Hope's dark hair as she looked expectantly at her father.

"What is it, Daniel?" Mother asked, looking up.

"Elder Brewster and Governor Bradford have decided on a week of thanksgiving. We are to invite Massasoit and his braves, and we shall have games and feasting and a giving of thanks to God for all the great things He has blessed us with."

"Oh!" Hope and Patience gasped, clapping their hands.

Mother gave a small smile, saying sadly, "I am afraid I can do so little to help."

Father sat down gently next to her, taking her hand in his as he said, "My dear, we ask nothing of you but to enjoy a week of rest."

"Thanksgiving I can at least do," Mother said, smiling.

"And feasting!" Hope pronounced, waving a wooden spoon in the air. "You may participate in much feasting."

Mother laughed, while Patience fluttered about excitedly, crying, "Games? What sort of games, Goodman Ellison?"

"I am afraid it is games for the men to enjoy, my sunshine, such as exercising our muskets and rifles for enjoyment," Father said, putting an arm around her waist as he sat down, for Patience was now quite like a daughter to him and Mother.

Hope whisked a trencher in front of him as she cried, "But what about we girls, Father? Shan't we have some activities as well?"

Suddenly the kettle began to boil over, and Patience cried, "Oh, the corn!" As she hurried to take it off the fire, Father said, "I am quite sure there will be activities for girls to enjoy—besides cooking the food."

"Oh, dear me, such cooking!" Hope suddenly exclaimed, smacking her brow with her hand. "I entirely forgot about the cooking! If this shall be a feast, imagine all the food we must cook, Patience!"

Father smiled approvingly, affectionately patting Hope's shoulder as she hurriedly set about the meal on the table.

"But we will find time for the games," Patience replied calmly, unashamed of her childish desire for amusement.

"Indeed." Hope tossed her a smile, before declaring the welcomed fact that supper was ready.

A sharp wind blew around the cottage as Father said the blessing. Hope closed the door firmly when he had finished, blocking out the night that threatened to make its way into the home. It seemed apparent, however, that even the darkness and wailing of the night would not break the familial bonds that held fast the little group in the golden lamplight; for hardship had produced love that encircled the family in a grip stronger than one before, as a Love more profound than that provided the core for the sweet relationship felt between them all.

The morning the week of thanksgiving was to begin dawned with streaks of silvery gold darting across the paling sky. Mother insisted she ought to help, as Hope and Patience hurriedly stirred up a breakfast of pottage just before sunrise, but Hope was inclined to be severe with her, commanding she stay in bed. Mother smiled at her strictness, but obeyed the orders Hope gave her and remained quietly in the cottage.

With the relief of Mother off her mind, Hope poured all her energy into the cooking, rather enjoying the challenge to prepare such a large meal by dinnertime. Priscilla had taken charge, instructing the other women on what needed to be done, so the time flew by as Hope rushed from one task to the other. The sun climbed higher and higher in the blue sky, until a sudden exclamation from Patience, who sat plucking a turkey on the threshold, brought several curious younger women to the door.

It was the Indians, a large troop of them, striding solemnly out of the woods with their chief, Massasoit, in the lead. Squanto and Father greeted them. After a few words of explanation, a gun salute was fired from the watch tower above the common house. Patience jumped. Hope covered her ears at the crack of the muskets above, but the other women continued their cooking and the young girls followed their example.

And so the sun rose higher and higher until it was pinned overhead, shining brightly down upon the bustling little colony and announcing to the busy women that it was time for the noon day meal. The feast was ready.

Elder Brewster sat at the head of a long table, and Massasoit sat at the foot, while the leaders of the colony and the leaders of the tribe lined along the side. Several more tables were scattered around in the crisp out-of-doors, containing the Indian braves and men of the congregation. Priscilla gently placed the last and largest turkey in front of Elder Brewster, while Hope and Patience and the other women stood to the side with bowed heads. After clearing his throat, Elder Brewster stood with a reverent look upon his face.

He began. "Our mighty Father; Thou hath blessed us with a bountiful harvest. We humbly thank Thee with grateful hearts the blessings Thou hath bestowed upon Thy children. Thou hath given us walls to shelter within, provisions to fulfill fleshly needs, and most of all, Father, Thou hath given us deep friendship with these neighbors who hath been kind and considerate toward we needy pilgrims. We thank Thee for a home—a land of freedom to worship Thee without hindrances that plagued us in England and Holland. Thou hath seen us over the seas and past illnesses to the place we stand to-day in reverent worship of *Thee*.

"Our earnest prayer, Father, is for our children, the future generations that might grow and live amongst these soils. We pray that Thy mighty hand might see them through hardships, trials, and transform them into beings that declare Thy wonderful glory.

"We thank Thee, Father, for Thy Son, for the sacrifice Thou hath abundantly given that we might see Thy shining face in the land of glory one day. There are many of our close relations whom we loved and cherished, who art standing in Thy matchless presence as we speak to Thee."

Elder Brewster paused, and Hope covered her mouth

with her hand, as tears streamed down her cheeks. *John.* But Elder Brewster hadn't finished, and he began again with a shaky voice, "Father, bless them. Bless us. We thank Thee, humbly, from the very depths of our hearts for the strength and courage Thou hath given us and all the goodness and blessings Thou hath bestowed upon us. Amen."

"Amen," Hope whispered, as many utterances of the same words were heard from the other members of the congregation.

Elder Brewster then began to carve the turkey, and eagerness shone on every face for the food to be eaten. But Hope did not feel as if she wished to eat, and she slipped away, darting around the common house, down toward where John's grave lay. She could not help the rush of tears that streamed down her cheeks, and she ran faster until she dropped to her knees by the old willow tree that bent soothingly over her sobbing form.

"John!" she wept, "John!" She buried her face in her apron, crying. A crisp autumn breeze whipped through, brushing a willow branch across her head and loosening her knotted hair behind.

"God, you have done so much!" she finally gasped out. "You took my brother, but You gave me Your Son. You took my homeland, but gave me this world of freedom." She tilted her tear-streaked face up to gaze into the brilliant blue sky. "You are so good!" she whispered. "You are so good!" She leaned back against a pine tree, watching the waving grasses rustle in the breeze, and closed her eyes as she felt the beautiful cool wind on her cheeks. She was overwhelmed.

But soon, as she discovered only a few short moments later, she had been unaware of another miracle taking place at that very instant. It was Patience who came running down the hill, her flyaway red hair tumbling behind her, shrieking to Hope the glad tidings. Hope paled and clutched her skirts with her hands as she allowed her sister to drag her up the hill, down the street, and to the doorway of the cottage.

A tiny wail burst through as Hope gingerly peeked in. Her eyes, after adjusting to the dim light, caught sight of Mother propped up in bed with a squirming bundle cuddled up in her arms. Goodwife Hopkins stood by with a bright smile on her good-natured face, while Father sat at the table with the worn leather Bible in hand. Hope at last ran inside, her face bursting into a grin. "Oh, Mother!" was all she could manage to say, and Mother gave her a loving smile.

"Come, dear," she said with a tired look on her thin face, "meet your new little sister."

"'Tis a girl?" Hope breathed, her hands clasped to her chest as she walked forward and knelt to look into the infant's pink face. A pair of blue eyes focused on her, and a little hand flew out, knocking Hope's cheek.

"Oh!" Hope breathed, pushing a strand of her tumbled hair behind her ear. "Oh, hallo, sweet child!" She reached out and hesitantly took the tiny hand in her own. To her delight, the fingers clung to her thumb while a squeal escaped the darling's lips.

Mother smiled. "Here, Hope." She began to hand the bundle to her daughter.

"Oh, no, Mother!" Hope cried in alarm, stepping back hastily. "You know how clumsy I am! Suppose she slips from my grasp?"

Mother laughed softly. "No, dear. You are no longer such a clumsy little girl. You are capable."

221

Hope felt tears fill her eyes.

"Come," Mother smiled tenderly, "take her into the warm sunshine just outside the doorway. I need some rest, and you ought to become acquainted with my little precious. She still needs a name—why do you and Patience not consider one?"

So Hope found herself taking the warm baby in her arms, cuddling it close to her shoulder as she stepped out into the noon light. Patience followed and closed the door behind her, and they sat down on the stoop carefully.

"Oh, Patience, I fear I will break the precious thing!" Hope gasped anxiously, gently laying the baby's head in the crook of her arm. The child blinked wonderingly in the sunlight, her blue eyes darting uncontrollably over the brilliant sky.

"You will not break her, Hope," Patience said with a giggle. "I think babies are stronger than most think."

"All the same," Hope replied doubtfully, clutching her sister tightly, "she is delicate. Oh!" she exclaimed, stroking the baby's soft cheek. "Oh, Patience, to think she was not in this world less than an hour ago—and now here she is, a new human emerged into this heartbreaking, beautiful life. How is that even possible, I wonder?"

"God is good," Patience said with conviction, leaning her chin on her knees. "I think He loves life even more than we do."

Hope gazed into the newborn's soft face, feeling the warm blanket squirm as the little body moved about inside of the swaddled cloths. "She is so tiny," she marveled. She touched her cheek.

Patience touched the little toes that peeked out. "What

is her name?" she asked, frowning.

Hope's forehead wrinkled up. "Elizabeth?" she suggested after some consideration.

Patience paled, and Hope, after glancing at her in alarm, answered her own question with a firm, "No."

They were all silent for a long moment until at last Patience, who had been sitting pensive the whole while, suggested quietly, "Endurance? We have endured a long, tragic winter and emerged victorious. It is elegant and beautiful, but more meaningful than any but our own congregation could presume."

"Oh!" Hope cried. "Oh, Patience, what a splendid name!" She looked down into the baby's face. "Endurance," she murmured, "your brother would have been proud to hold you." Her face crumpled, and she suddenly hugged the baby close. "As he cannot, I shall. I shall watch after you, sweet girl, as he cared for me. We shall stay together from now on." She looked into the baby's face, her eyes filling. "Precious little miracle."

Cry of Hope

CHAPTER XXIX
Familiar Strangers

Hope rocked little Endurance by the hearth one morning early in November. Singing softly to the baby, she stroked the warm little back. Endurance hiccuped.

Mother had gone up to Elder Brewster's cottage to help Goodwife Brewster sew winter clothes for her two growing little boys. Patience was off on another acorn expedition with Francis Billington and Constanta Hopkins, and Father was on duty in the watch tower.

The air had grown chilly now. Sharp winds blew, scattering dead leaves across the road and around the corners of the house. The sky was paler blue than it had been in the summer, and oftentimes the sun would be hidden behind white churning clouds that signaled winter's beginning.

But the cottage was pleasantly warm, the food was stored in the loft around and about Hope and Patience's beds, and the fact that her family was safe kept Hope in good spirits. The long winter of last year had burnt permanently in her mind, and she knew she would never have looked upon their provisions with such thankfulness if she had not been through such horrid experiences. Holding Endurance close in that peaceful moment, Hope breathed another prayer of thanksgiving, feeling grateful that the little child had been born after they were settled.

Suddenly a fast tramping of feet was heard at the door. Mother burst in with Patience close behind. One look at their pale faces brought Hope rising from her seat in an instant, clutching Endurance to her shoulder. "What is it?" she asked tensely. Mother hurried forward to take the baby while Hope stood frozen.

Patience looked at her a moment before whispering, "A ship has been spotted."

The room grew deathly silent.

Hope's face paled. She stood alarmingly still for a moment; then she ran out the door. The sharp winter wind pummeled her face, reddening her cheeks, as she scrambled up the hill. She paid no mind to the worried, anxious, or excited looks of her fellow villagers. She darted into the common house and up to the watch tower.

It was crowded with the men of the militia that had been hastily thrown together the year before. The wide windows offered majestic views of the ocean below, and Hope ran to one, leaning her arms on the ledge and staring at the vast body of water. Indeed, a speck lay upon the surface in the distance. It was a ship, to be sure, and Hope buried her face in her hands, far too overcome to think.

Suddenly a hand rested gently on her shoulder, and she turned, finding Joshua gazing down upon her. She wiped her red eyes and smiled. He leaned out the window, his musket

225

firmly clutched upon his shoulder, and she felt glad he was there with her.

"Did you ever hope for something you feared would not come to pass?" she asked him tremulously, staring hard with watery eyes at the tiny ship upon the horizon.

Joshua nodded slowly, swallowing. "Yes. That is where trust enters, I suppose. If it is to happen, it will happen. If it is not, it will not. In the end, He knows best, despite our... despite our wishes." He seemed reluctant to say the words, as if a hope of his own weighed upon his heart so heavily that he did not wish to let it go.

Hope leaned her cheek on her hand, gazing out into wind. A breeze blew, whipping her hair around her face. "Oh, how I *hope* Constance is on the ship," she breathed, tears stinging the corners of her eyes.

"There is nothing we can do but wait," Joshua replied, draping his arms over the ledge as his sharp hazel eyes swept over the view before them.

So they waited. And as they waited, Hope's mind wandered back through the year past. Images, burnt in her mind so strong they were, stirred up. The intense love and longing piercing from Constance's eyes the day they said farewell. The question she had never answered John when he asked whether she would set her heart on the past or the future. John himself—the look that burned in his eyes when speaking of the country they would help found, the brotherly love he gently showed when around her, the steadfast faith he genuinely owned. Then Joshua—the companionship he never backed down on, his steady heart and mind, the capable hands that worked through pain and hardship, the dependable atmosphere that continually surrounded him.

She took a deep breath, looking out at the land before her.

The country. The land that was filled with abundance if man would only trouble himself to dig it out. The large blue skies, full of clearer air that any Hope had ever known, smelling sweeter than any fresh scents found in Holland. The rolling golden grasses at the end of summer, the blankets of soft snow in winter, the bright green leaves that burst forth in spring, the crisp, colourful enhances that graced autumn. The trees that swept her ears with the soothing sound of rustling leaves in the breeze. The grass that tickled the bottoms of her feet. The plants that grew in the soft, fertile earth. The sky, intense and wide with the depth of immeasurable atmosphere. The awe-striking echoes—from the rocks to the hills to the valleys—the echoes that shouted of freedom. Her heart felt as if could burst from her chest with love that radiated within her. Her green eyes grew brighter and brighter, staring into space as the thoughts and emotions seared through. But suddenly a bellow awoke her.

She shook herself, glancing around. Everyone—from the women and children in the street below to the men of the militia on watch around her—everyone was cheering, shrieking, or crying. "Oh!" she cried, grasping Joshua's arm. "Oh, what is it?"

He smiled at her. "Did you not hear? Ah, I thought you were in a daze. 'Tis an English ship! Look at the fair flag!"

Hope's eyes widened until they flashed even greener with the excitement blazing inside of her. Her clutch on his arm grew tighter and tighter as she stared at the beautiful blue and red and white colours radiating from the ship that seemed to shine like a beacon upon the waters. "Oh!" she gasped, trembling. "Oh!" And, unable to contain the emotions inside of her, she buried her face in Joshua's shoulder and cried.

Upon lifting her tear-streaked face, she found him smiling down upon her, a look of simple satisfaction written across his honest face. She smiled back, laughed, and twirled around, feeling lighter than air. However, of a sudden she stopped, her face paling. "Oh, but Constance may not be on it," she said, covering her mouth.

"Then we shall find out," Joshua said firmly, shouldering his musket and taking her hand.

He led her down to the beach, where the cool summer sea had changed into a choppy winter ocean, its frigid water sweeping over the sand before slipping back into the depths. Hope shivered and sat down on a rock, tucking her feet under her skirt. Joshua settled next to her, laying his musket across his knees. All was silent for a moment, but soon another step was heard, and Patience came.

Sitting cross-legged—a trait she had picked up from Squanto—on the opposite side of Hope, she stared at the ship with her unreadable dark eyes. Her pale face was pinched, and she looked so anxious that Hope put an arm around her, saying fondly, "What is wrong, dear sister?"

Patience squirmed, and Hope looked at her in surprise. Her sister's cheeks were flushed, and she clutched a strand of curly red hair as she always did when agitated. She glanced at her with an uncertain expression a moment before saying softly, "You and Constance were always such good friends. Somehow I managed to bestow very good reasons for the both of you to keep your distance from me. I wish... Rather, I *hope*..." She trailed off, her cheeks flushed.

Hope broke into a smile, and she impulsively flung her arms around her. "You and she and I shall be sisters. I promise. Do you brighten under that prospect?"

Patience's face cleared then, and she nodded. "Do you suppose she is aboard the ship?" she asked, squinting at its shadow upon the sea.

Hope's face fell once again. "I do not know." Upon looking out at the ocean, she felt she could not bear to wait for it to inch its way closer to shore.

Silence fell upon all three of them sitting upon the rock. They said not another word for nearly an hour, when at last Hope leapt to her feet, for she could spot the voyagers waving from the deck. "Oh!" she cried, straining her eyes. "Oh, I cannot see the faces! Oh, I wish they *would* hurry!" She trembled with excitement. "Oh! Oh, look! They are coming! They are coming!" She watched breathlessly as a small boat was lowered into the water. She nearly tumbled into the ocean herself as she peered at the faint outlines of the people filling the boat studying it until she thought her eyes would burst. At last the boat came rowing to shore. Hope's heart thudded in her ears, and she felt as if she could break with impatience and anxiety.

With each ocean wave, the boat drew nearer. Now Hope could see the waving caps and hear the shouts of greetings. Her throat felt hot, and she wiped her clammy hands on her skirt over and over, praying that Constance would be with the little group. Steadily, the boat came nearer. It came nearer. Now Hope could see the faces of the passengers. Her eyes darted from one to another. There were ruddy-faced men, a few anxious women, and then—suddenly a shrill shriek burst from her lips. A slim, rosy face was peeking out, waving frantically to Hope, the blue eyes so familiar and kind. Constance's face burst into a beautiful grin, and Hope collapsed into tears, hugging herself with joy.

The boat bumped onto the rock that Hope stood upon. The crowd of people came swarming out, and Hope felt rather lost among them when suddenly she came face-to-face with her friend. She stood frozen a moment, her eyes staring into Constance's soft blue ones. Then she flung herself into her friend's arms, and they laughed, crying. For a long moment, they stood embracing one another, for what they thought could have been lost was found once again, and they could not bear to let the other out of their grasp for an instant.

But at length Constance took a step back and cried, "Oh, Hope, you have grown! In that short year and a half you have become a woman."

Hope laughed, wiping tears from her eyes, and said, "I could say the same for you. You have grown so tall—and so slender! You are quite taller than I now, while you used to be the round rosy-faced little girl."

Constance smiled.

They stood staring at one another, seemingly unable to believe the other was the same as they used to be. Suddenly a woman stepped from the crowd, squeezing Constance's shoulder.

"Oh, Hope!" Constance said suddenly. "This is my mother."

Hope stared at Constance a moment. Constance gazed back at her with joy in her eyes, and Hope then held her hand out to the sunny-haired lady, saying warmly, "Ah, I am so pleased to meet you! I know Constance loves you dearly."

The woman smiled, her blue eyes twinkling. "I know

that Constance loves *you* dearly. She has spoken so often of you. You simply must introduce me to your family—your kind parents and brother."

Hope froze. *John.* Her spirits crumpled again to the ground, and she began to again feel the intense pain of loss. She looked down at her shoes, uttering a prayer silently almost before realizing it. She took a shaky breath, looking up. "John died," she whispered.

Constance's mouth dropped, her blue eyes widening.

"It broke my heart," Hope said steadily, "but it has healed. God healed it." Her eyes drifted up to the broad blue sky, and a faint smile settled on her lips, unexpected to both her and her observers.

Constance silently watched her a moment until at last she seemed to grasp the meaning of Hope's words. She reached out to give her a silent embrace, whispering, "I prayed He would find you."

Hope smiled. "I thought you might have."

CHAPTER XXX

Hope

Hope sat on the floor of the cottage. Her family had gathered in their home's warm haven at the first sign of evening's approach. Father and Mother were earnestly talking with Constance's mother. Patience fluttered about, sometimes stoking the fire, sometimes leaning on Father's shoulder, sometimes sitting on the floor by Hope and Constance. The excitement brought out the flighty spirit within her, and her mood matched the flyaway red hair which Hope fondly told her fitted her personality exactly.

Constance and Hope chattered away merrily. The old friends had not grown apart, for the bond that had glued them together during childhood still lived out its strength in their new-found womanhood. Constance held little Endurance close, for she had always been motherly as a little girl and now proved she had lived up to the capabilities, for she seemed to have a secret touch that soothed the baby immensely.

Constance understood the transformation of Patience from Hope's former "enemy" to becoming her friend. Hope's letter had revealed that fact to her, and she unknowingly reached out with her cheerful spirit, drawing Patience in with the subconscious face of friendship.

Indeed, the room had taken upon an even pleasanter feel now that Constance and her mother had joined the group, and Hope felt her heart swell with joy, which brought unshed tears to her eyes every now and again.

In the midst of excited plans on having Constance and her mother stay with them during the winter, a rap was heard at the door. Hope, being closest, opened it, finding Joshua standing outside with cheeks ruddy from the crisp breezes. "Good evening," he said with a cordial nod, which was so formal Hope laughed outright. He smiled at the pretty picture of the family encircled around the fire and addressed Hope's father. "Can you spare your daughter for a short while? I thought I would ask her for a walk."

Father came to the door and watched him closely a moment, his eyes darting from Hope's flushed cheeks to Joshua's steady hazel eyes and back again. Finally he said, "Indeed. Promise me you will never leave her side, son, and you may go."

"I promise, sir," Joshua said, shaking his hand and looking him in the eye. "With all of my heart."

Father's hand lingered in his firm clasp a moment, until Joshua and Hope were suddenly walking down the street together toward the water that reflected the sunset's short lasting splendor of golds and silvers. A few sentences passed between them: Hope's short eager words speaking of seeing Constance, and Joshua's quiet voice mentioning the cooling weather. However, upon reaching the beach, a silence enveloped them; yet it was a comfortable silence. It was a silence of harmonious heartbeat evolved after years of friendship and growing fondness. It was a silence that seemed to speak something that words could never communicate. It was a silence quivering with hope.

Hope bent and scooped a handful of sand in her palm, letting it slip through her fingertips. "You know," she said softly, "while gazing at the land in the watch tower, I think my heart finally found this country."

"Did it?"

"Yes; and I have no regrets. I belong here—where freedom rings from the crevices of the rocks to the leaves of the trees. Finding Christ showed and gave me the freedom I craved. If this land gives me the earthly freedom not found in other countries, then in this land I stay."

Joshua gazed down at her, his eyes glistening in the sunset light.

Suddenly she straightened and stepped to the rock she had stepped upon when the shallop first bumped against shore. Closing her eyes, she felt the cool breeze whip across her face, reflecting the wild echoes of freedom in the land. She opened her arms, taking in the beauty of life itself with a heart open as the peace and hope of God's love and grace rushed in, filling her up to the highest capacity until she felt more content than when she first laid eyes on Constance again. She stood there silently for a long moment until a voice from behind said tremulously, "Hope."

She stood still a moment. A tremor rippled through her veins at the tender tone of his voice, and she wondered why her heart seemed to know what he was to say before she turned and saw the look on his face.

Stepping forward, he whispered, "*Noe wammaw ause,*

Hope."

    She slowly looked up at him, and her eyes locked with his. "I love you," she said softly. She held out her slim hand, and he took it with his strong one, clasping it.

    "Hope," he said with a reflective smile, "the day before your brother died, when you thought he was to be well... he knew he was to die. He told me so, and during that time, he asked me to watch out for you—to protect you as a brother." He stopped, looking down at the small hand held in his own. "I would rather protect you as a husband," he said softly, "and then... then watch out for you always." He looked searchingly in her green eyes that were filling involuntarily. "In a few years, Hope, when you are older, and I have more to give you... would you become my wife?"

    She felt a catch in her throat and stood for a moment, looking down. Her heart burned, aching with love that she had never felt nor known nor chosen before, but in a moment, flinging her head up, she said with a smile through tears that streamed down her face, "I know I would."

    His face burst into a grin.

    The sunset had disappeared, leaving a cool twilight that enveloped the two figures on the beach. As Hope stood softly by Joshua's side, her hand clasped in his, a bright star appeared on the horizon shining with a steady, unchanging light. It was, as John said, a beautiful symbol of hope; and in her heart, Hope knew that, despite the struggles the future may bring her, she would evermore have that hope—for now she had the faith of the Truth to keep it safely within her.

Glossary

DUTCH

goedendag – good day
hoe ga je vergaat? – how are you faring?
ik zal je missen – I'll miss you
ja – yes
lieve vriend – dear friend
nu, nu, op te vrolijken, zon! – now, now, cheer up, sunshine!

WAMPANOAG

netop – a friend
nicksquaw – a maid
nitka – a mother
noeshow – a father
noe wammaw ause – I love you

Acknowledgements

The struggles I went through creating this story are rather numerable, but it amazes me seeing it brought together at last. That being said, I cannot forget to thank those very important persons in my life who helped bring to life this dream implanted in my heart.

    Momma, you were ever ready to listen to my complaints and despairs during the writing stage of my story. It meant more to me than anything. Daddy, your theological assistance has not been forgotten, and I truly thank you for your encouragement and excitement throughout this process. Caleb, Sam, Anna, Katie, and Elisha: each and every one of you have influenced the course of my life, which in turn influences my writing life. I couldn't ask for better (or cooler) siblings. Nana and Papa, your continuous belief in my abilities aided my spirits when they were low, and I am so grateful for your love and support. Mimi and Grampa, you somehow managed to see a smidgen of talent in my earliest writings, and your encouragement to pursue it didn't fall on deaf ears. Uncle Patrick, at least a quarter of the writing of this book was spent at the desk you built for me (the other half was on my bed, and the other quarter was in the car coming home from Nana's house). I just thought you'd like to know.

To my beta-readers, Emily Putzke and Anne Marie Gosnell. Em, you're one of my best friends, and I am so blessed to have met you. Thanks so much for your help. I love you so much! Mrs. Anne Marie, I thank you from the depths of my heart for your editing suggestions and your excitement concerning my book. I love you and your crazy family!

Mr. Henley, you are truly a blessing. I honestly look at you as another grandfather, and your talented work on the cover made my year. Mrs. Duffy, exchanging babysitting duties for formatting is probably the best barter I've ever taken part in. Thank you so much; I am incredibly blessed to know you!

Violetta Miller: you're face is Hope's face. Really, I thank you for being the beautiful model for Mr. Henley to work with, and I hope you are blessed by this book.

Most importantly, I thank You, God. Thank You for placing all these beautiful people in my life to piece this book together. If it hadn't been for Your loving, guiding hand, this book would never have reached the emotional impact and the portrayal of the truth that it did. Your gift of writing is one of the best things You could ever have given me. I love You.

About The Author

Emily Chapman is a homeschooled student living with her parents and four siblings in the southeastern United States. With a thirst for stories and creativity, she not only writes, but enjoys exercising her imagination through dance and photography. She believes in running through sprinklers in the summertime, watching the Andy Griffith show, listening to country music, and traversing to Narnia. But above all, she is saved through faith by the Son of the Creator and is adopted into God's family of beautiful souls.

YAF 3GPL000100219Z
CHA *Chapman, Emily.*
PB   *Cry Of Hope*

GALLATIN PUBLIC LIBRARY
GALLATIN, TENNESSEE

9061679R00142

Made in the USA
San Bernardino, CA
05 March 2014